Born in 1968 in Niodior, Senegal, **Fatou Diome** moved to Strasbourg in 1994. She has taught at Strasbourg University and currently presents a cultural programme on the television station FR3. She is the author of a collection of short stories called *La Préférence Nationale*. *The Belly of the Atlantic* is her first novel.

Praise for *The Belly of the Atlantic*

'When it comes to immigration, clichés abound.
Fatou Diome's first novel sweeps them all away. This
well-written saga grips the reader and confronts prejudice'
Le Figaro

'Fatou Diome confirms her enormous talent with this
powerful, epic novel' *Le Canard Enchainé*

'It's the humour of the book that entices the reader to want
to know more about its author… *The Belly of the Atlantic* is a
great read – unputdownable' *Le Monde*

A complete catalogue record for this book can be
obtained from the British Library on request

The right of Fatou Diome to be identified as the author
of this work has been asserted by her in accordance with the
Copyright, Designs and Patents Act 1988

First published as *Le Ventre de l'Atlantique* by
Editions Anne Carrière, Paris, 2003

First published in 2006 by Serpent's Tail,
4 Blackstock Mews, London N4 2BT
www.serpentstail.com

Designed and typeset by Sue Lamble
Printed by MacKays of Chatham plc

ISBN 978-1-85242-903-4
ISBN-13 1-85242-903-8

The Belly of the Atlantic

Fatou Diome

Translated by Lulu Norman and Ros Schwartz

I would like to thank le Centre National du Livre
for its help and support

To my grandparents, my beacons

To Bineta Sarr, my mother, my African sister.
Now I imagine you finally at rest, taking tea
With Muhammed and Simone de Beauvoir.
I lay my wreaths of words down here,
So my freedom may be yours.

1

HE RUNS, TACKLES, DRIBBLES, STRIKES, falls, gets up again, carries on running. Faster! But the wind's changed: now the ball's heading straight for the crotch of Toldo, the Italian goalie. Oh God, do something! I'm not shouting, I'm begging you: if you're the Almighty, do something! Ah, back comes Maldini, his legs knitting up the turf.

In front of the TV, I leap off the sofa and give a violent kick. Ouch, the table! I wanted to run with the ball, help Maldini get it back, shadow him halfway down the pitch so he could bury it in the back of the opponent's net. But all my kick did was spill my cold tea onto the carpet. At this exact moment I imagine the Italians tensing up, stiff as the human fossils of Pompeii. I still don't know why they clench their buttocks when the ball nears the goal.

'Maldini! Oh yes, great defending from Maldini, who passes to his keeper! And Toldo kicks it away. What a talent, this Maldini! A truly great player. Still staying loyal to AC Milan. Over a hundred caps for Italy! Amazing. Cesare, his father, was a fine player too; the family definitely has talent!'

The commentator would have liked to make up a poem in praise of Maldini, but in the heat of the moment he could only utter a string of exclamations.

Why am I telling you all this? Because I adore football?

Not that much. Why, then? Because I'm in love with Maldini? No way! I'm not that crazy. I'm not starstruck. I don't crane my neck gazing up at the sky. My grandma taught me early on how to pick up stars: all you have to do is place a basin of water in the middle of the yard at night and they'll be at your feet. Try it yourself, you only need a small dish in the corner of the garden to see twenty-two stars, Maldini among them, chasing round in circles on the grass like rats in a maze. So, since I'm not writing Maldini a love letter, why am I telling you all this? Simply because not all viruses land you in hospital. Some just work inside us like they do in a computer program and cause breakdown.

It's 29 June 2000 and I'm watching the European Cup. It's Italy *v.* Holland in the semi-final. My eyes are staring at the TV, but my heart's contemplating other horizons.

Over there, people have been clinging to a scrap of land, the island of Niodior, for centuries. Stuck to the gum of the Atlantic like bits of leftover food, they wait resignedly for the next big wave that will either carry them off or leave them their lives. This thought hits me every time I retrace my path and my memory glimpses the minaret of the mosque, rigid in its certainties, and the coconut palms, shaking their hair in a nonchalant pagan dance whose origin is forgotten. Is it one of those ancient funeral dances that sanctifies the reunion of our dead with our ancestors? Or the oft-repeated one that celebrates marriages at the end of the harvest, after the rainy season? Or even that third kind of dance sparked by storms, during which, they say, the coconut palms imitate the shudder of young girls given in marriage to men they don't love? The fourth is the most mysterious, the dream tango, and everyone has their own version that follows the rhythm of their breathing.

It's nearly ten years since I left the shade of the coconut palms. Pounding the asphalt, my imprisoned feet recall their former liberty, the caress of warm sand, being nipped by crabs and the little thorn pricks that remind you there's life even in the body's forgotten extremities. I tread European ground, my feet sculpted and marked by African earth. One step after another, it's the same movement all humans make, all over the planet. Yet I know my western walk has nothing in common with the one that took me through the alleys, over the beaches, paths and fields of my native land. People walk everywhere, but never towards the same horizon. In Africa, I followed in destiny's wake, between chance and infinite hopefulness. In Europe, I walk down the long tunnel of efficiency that leads to well-defined goals. Here, chance plays no part; every step leads to an anticipated result and hope is measured by appetite for the fight. In the Technicolor world, you walk differently, towards an internalised destiny you set yourself regardless, without ever realising, for you're pressed into the modern mob, caught up in the social steamroller ready to crush all those who dare pull over onto the hard shoulder. So, under the grey European sky, or in unexpected sunlight, I walk on, counting my steps, each one bringing me closer to my dream. But how many kilometres, how many work-filled days and sleepless nights still separate me from that so-called success that my people, on the other hand, took for granted from the moment I told them I was leaving for France? I walk on, my steps weighed down by their dreams, my head filled with my own. I walk on and have no idea where I'll end up. I don't know which mast the flag of victory is hoisted on, nor which waters could wash away the stain of failure. Hey, you, don't nod off; my head's boiling over! Pass me the wood! This fire needs stoking. Writing's my witch's cauldron; at night I brew up dreams too tough to cook.

The noise of the television shakes me from my reverie. Every time the commentators shout Maldini's name, a face fills the screen. Thousands of kilometres from my sitting room, on the other side of the earth, in Senegal, on that island barely big enough to accommodate a stadium, I picture a young man glued to a battered old TV set, watching the same match as me. I feel him next to me. Our eyes meet on the same images. Hearts thudding, gasps, outbursts of joy or despair, all our emotions are synchronised while the match plays, because we're right behind the same man: Paolo Maldini.

So, over there, at the ends of the earth, I see a young man on a mat or an old bench stamping his feet in front of an ancient TV, which, despite its sputtering, commands as big an audience as a cinema screen. The owner of the only TV in the area generously sets it up in his yard and all the neighbours flock unannounced. The place is open to everyone; the sex, age and number of spectators vary according to the programme. This afternoon, 29 June 2000, the weather's good, the sky's a perfect blue and the TV isn't crackling, even if the owner had to bang it with his fist to get it going. The eyes trained on it have all the freshness of innocence. Boys in the flower of youth, their bodies formed by long years of running after balls made of rags, then unhoped-for footballs, jostle and press together, liquid energy streaming down their smooth foreheads. Alert to every move, they yell out their predictions.

One of the young men is silent, concentrated on the images. He leans towards the screen; his gaze weaves among the heads. Jaw clenched, only the odd jerky movement betrays the passion inside him. At Maldini's first tackle, his foot spontaneously strikes the bum of the boy squatting in front of him, hoofing him into the air. The victim turns round in fury but, seeing the guilty party's face utterly engrossed, doesn't count on an apology and finds a place a little further off. You don't step on a blind man's balls twice, the saying goes: once is enough for him to pick up his merchandise as soon as he hears the sound of footsteps. The boy should shift his arse anyway, because the match was only just beginning and there'd be many more exciting moments. Already it's enough to make you commit hara-kiri: a red card for Zambrota, the Italian number 17. That's too much for the young man. As frustrated as Dino Zoff, the Italian coach, he straightens up and mutters something the ref wouldn't have liked. You get it: he supports the Italians and from now on you're not allowed to support any other team, out of respect. Fate really is against them: a yellow card for Francesco Toldo, the Italian keeper, who just grabbed hold of the Dutch number 9. The young man stands up, clutching his head in his hands, waiting for the inevitable punishment which soon follows: penalty against Italy.

Do something, God! I should stop shouting? No, but you've no idea! It's not important? Of course it's important! Yes, I know, it's not Hiroshima. If that was all, I couldn't care less, but don't you see they might score a goal that will break Madické's heart! Who's Madické? Who's Madické? You think I've got time to tell you that? A penalty's not a coffee break; it rips out as fast as a footballer's fart! So are you going to do something or what? What about all my prayers, what about Ramadan? You think I do all that for nothing?

Toldo, the Italian goalie, saves it. Madické gives a violent kick, but this time no one's in the way. Phew! We've avoided the worst. His chest heaves with a long sigh, he relaxes, and his face lights up with a smile I know won't last. The match goes on.

Every time the Italians make a mistake, he puts his hands together in prayer. Just before half-time, Maldini argues with the ref's decision and is rewarded with a yellow card. Madické's smile's wiped off his face; he knows a second yellow card is the same as a red and his idol will be sent off.

He squeezes his head in his hands with worry: he doesn't want to see his hero relegated to the sidelines. He'd like to talk to him, tell him the tactics he's devising, right there on his bench. Short of playing alongside him, he'd like to lend Maldini his legs, so he'd have a spare pair. But there, on that bench, his feet burrowing in the white, burning sand, how many dream kilometres separate him from the traces of mud Maldini will leave in the dressing rooms at half-time?

Transforming his despair into dialogue, he screams words that catch in the tops of the Niodior palms, never to reach Maldini's ears. I'm his devoted messenger: Madické and I have the same mother. People who only love by halves will tell you he's my half-brother, but to me he's my little brother and that's that.

So tell Maldini his yellow or red cards are too much to bear, they're crushing my heart. Tell him to save his skin, stay in one piece, not land a ball in the face, not let the opposition mow him down. Tell him I groan every time he cops it. Tell him his hot breath is searing my lungs. Tell him I feel his injuries and bear the scars. Tell him above all that I saw him, in Niodior, chasing the bubble of a dream over the warm sand. Because one day, on waste ground, my brother turned into Maldini. So tell Maldini about his wrestler's body, his dark eyes, his frizzy hair, his gorgeous smile and white teeth. That Maldini is my little brother, swallowed up in his dream.

The ref blows the half-time whistle, the young spectators make for the tree opposite the house, partly to stretch their legs but also to argue more loudly without disturbing their host. Only Madické stays by the house. He wouldn't miss the second half for the world. Nothing but ads on the TV now. Even in these regions, where drinking water's still a luxury, Coca-Cola brazenly comes to swell its sales figures. Have no fear, Coca-Cola will make the Sahel wheat grow! The TV attracts a group of scrawny seven- to ten-year-olds, their only playthings the sticks of wood and tins they've picked up in the street, who burst out laughing at the ad's suggestive scene: a boy approaches a group of girls who seem to be ignoring him. He offers a Coke to the prettiest one and beckons to her; the girl, after a refreshing gulp, generously offers him her waist. He puts his arm around her and they leave together, smiling. The boys guffaw. One asks another: 'What's he going to do to her?'

The others snigger. The apparent leader of the gang answers, digging him with his elbow: 'You stupid or what? He's going to screw her.'

Encouraged by the leader, another boy goes on: 'They're having a dance at the back of my house. I saw my big brother and his friends bring cases of Coca-Cola. Wahey! The girls are going to get what's coming to them!'

The laughter breaks out louder than ever. Now it's Miko's turn to whet their appetites. An enormous ice-cream cone, colours glistening, fills the screen, then a chubby little boy appears, greedily licking a huge ice cream. Envious purrs replace the inanity of a moment ago: a chorus of 'Mmm! Oooh! That's good! Mmm!' These kids know ice cream only through images. For them it's a virtual food, eaten only *over there*, on the other side of the Atlantic, in the paradise where that plump kid had the good sense to be born. But they're crazy for that ice cream; for its sake they've memorised the advertising schedule. They chant the word 'Miko', repeat it the way believers intone their holy book. They look forward to this ice cream as Muslims look forward to the paradise of Muhammad, and come here to await it like Christians awaiting the return of Christ. They've found icons for this Miko cone; they've made rough sculptures out of bits of wood, painted them with red and yellow crayons to represent mouthwatering ice creams. And it's these sticks of wood they sniff now as they savour the ad. I dream of a Miko swimming pool, built in the name of pleasure, not turnover. They dream of devouring this ice cream as Madické dreams of shaking Maldini's hand.

The ads draw to an end. The older boys, who were arguing about the match under the tree, gather in front of the television again and shoo away the younger boys, who are too noisy. Elders are respected around here. An old fisherman, still strong, dressed in rags, makes himself comfortable right in front of Madické, who identifies him by the smell of fish penetrating his nostrils. Greetings are polite but brief. That smell is fetid but respect shuts you up. Madické keeps quiet. He knows that in these parts the decades you've accumulated are aces that trump everything. He'll have to put up with this putrefying fossil for the whole of the second half. So he concentrates and imagines he's over there, where the match is being played, far from the old fisherman.

The stadium reappears. The players aren't out of the dressing rooms yet, but the commentators are warming up, and Maldini's name keeps being mentioned. What are they saying about him? Madické wonders. He strains to hear; it's not easy with his neighbours commentating the match like seasoned experts. He leans in nearer to the flickering screen, cups his ear in his hand as if better to isolate himself from the group, and listens again. The commentators' voices are slightly more audible, but the language they use flies past his ears without really going in. It's so annoying! And that smell, too, getting stronger and stronger…Only Maldini's name reaches him clearly at odd intervals. But what the hell are they saying about him?

And yet he's often heard, even seen, that language. Yes, he's seen it, here in his country: that language wears trousers, suits, ties, shoes with laces; or skirts, suits, sunglasses and high heels. He does recognise the language that flows in Senegalese offices, but he doesn't understand it and that irritates him. The second half begins.

The first free kick goes to the Italians. Madické's delighted. They've pulled themselves together, he thinks, and that reassures him. But his optimism's soon frustrated. The Dutch value their honour. They defend their goal like a nun defends her fanny. The Italians have to deal with it. This sublimated war on the turf demands nerves of steel, and it's not easy holding out for ninety minutes. Especially in these last moments of the match when every move counts. Madické sweats; it's hot, and, besides, that stink of fish is beginning to turn his stomach.

The ref whistles an end to the ninety minutes; the adversaries will have to wait for extra time to fight on. Although their thirst for glory keeps them on their feet, their ravaged faces beg for rest. Like a protective mother, a sister moved to tears or a devoted wife, I'd like to offer them a drink, sponge their faces, bandage their cuts and give them a hug. I'd like to tell them their frustrating match is like life: the best goals are always yet to come; it's just that waiting for them is painful.

Covered in mud and streaming with sweat, the players huddle together, their shoulders slumped, crushed by so much fruitless effort.

Rest before extra time. The group of young spectators who've stayed in front of the television becomes animated. The match is upsetting their forecasts. The nervous ones are keen to assert their point of view, waving their hands about. The advertising jingles ring out. The kids from before rush over. The old fisherman picks a quarrel to kill time; with a teasing smile, he taps Madické on the shoulder and, stroking his beard, says: 'What's happening? Maldini, eh? Eh? Not up to it today, huh? Your opponents are looking pretty solid.'

Madické looks up at the man before fixing his eyes on the dusk-filled horizon. There's something disarming in silence, in knowledge, too. The old man's feeling inspired and won't back down. Coming over all learned, he keeps preening his beard and utters a deep thought that's just occurred to him: 'You know, Maldini, the greater the obstacle you overcome, the more dazzling your success. The quality of the victory depends on the merit of the opposition. Beating a coward doesn't make a man a hero.'

This rambling is hardly a consolation to Madické. He's heard this Neanderthal philosophy before – this exotic verbiage, falsified a thousand times, dumped on us by westerners, the better to sideline us. Enough already with all these convenient proverbs. Didn't the old fisherman know, conversely, that losing to a brave adversary doesn't make a man a hero either?

The sun seemed to flee human questioning and threatened to plunge into the Atlantic. The sky, fired up with passion, looked lower than usual, leaving a hanging trail of reddish light over the tops of the coconut palms. The sea breeze, in its mercy, brushed the skin almost imperceptibly. Only a few women on their way back from the well, late with their domestic chores, noticed the dusk's light wind, which swept under their cotton *pagnes* to caress them where the sun never sees. It was devoted women such as these, too, who dared disturb the village's incipient calm with the last pounding of their pestles. Thump! Thump! Thump! These pestles, distant and repetitive, reverberated in the depths of Madické's heart. Because he'd heard them all his life, he recognised them, could even decode them: they always precede the call of the muezzin and the owls' song. For all the islanders they've become the music that heralds the night. But in this superstitious universe, they also mark the hour of the evil spirits and the moment ancestral fears slip into the shadows.

When, as a kid, he'd hear the pounding of the pestles,

Madické would leave the improvised playgrounds, following his friends, and run back to our mother. He knew exactly where to find her: she was always in her kitchen at this hour, at the far end of the back yard, busy cooking supper or grinding a fistful of millet to make the milk curd porridge for the next day. If by some unhappy chance she wasn't there, he'd take his little bench and settle down in the kitchen in front of the fire, to avoid his dread of the creeping shadows outside. Impatiently, he'd stave off his boredom by feeding wood to the fire, marvelling at the dancing flames until a voice, feigning severity, reached his ears.

'Hey, stop that, Madické! What a blaze you're making! You'll burn my supper!'

Time had passed. The uneasy atmosphere of dusk still drove him to seek the reassurance of skirts, but no longer his mother's. In any case, on this 29 June 2000 the most beguiling of nymphs couldn't have held his gaze.

The magical curtain of ads is torn. The younger boys scatter, echoing the last notes of their favourite song: Miko! Miko! Sunk in black, the yard looks like a marine graveyard. Only the bluish glow from the old television weakly illuminates the spectators' faces. The silence is proper for contemplation. The muezzin yells himself hoarse for nothing. He'll just have to have some mint tea afterwards; it'll do him good! The stadium reappears, the faithful cheer their gods. The old fisherman noisily clears his throat, shakes his neighbour's arm and announces, as if confiding in him: 'Maldini, my son, the moment of truth is upon us.'

Madické gives the requisite faint smile before taking his arm back, irritated by a foul by Jaap Stam, a Dutch player.

'Red card!' he yells.

But the ref's satisfied with a yellow.

'Shit, he should've got a red card! That ref's a right b—'

The sentence is left unfinished; no one knows where

anger will end. The Dutch are undeterred. They're more and more audacious. Aron Winter makes his point forcefully and wins a corner. Eighty-four caps earns you a lot of experience, especially in cheating. Seedorf fancies himself to take the corner. Delvecchio rushes forward, proving to his mum that her milk wasn't wasted: she definitely suckled a hero, capable of restoring hope to the entire Italian nation. But the Dutch mothers have done the same, and their sons, eager to make them proud, go back on the attack. Cannavaro blocks and gets it away; Maldini sprints off. Madické peels off his bench, imagining he's right behind him: 'Come on! Go for it! You can do it! Go!' he shouts, practically rupturing his vocal cords.

Everything you want, you've got it!

A cousin who'd been deported from the USA never stopped listening to that song and translated it for anyone who wanted to hear: where there's a will there's a way. Madické's beginning to have his doubts, and justifiably so.

The two periods of extra time remain goalless. Now a penalty shoot-out's inevitable. Madické knows this, and his heart's beating wildly in his breast. He presses his hand to it but that doesn't help; the palpitations increase.

The mistress of the house calls everyone for supper. The meal here isn't reserved for those who live in the house; everyone who's around when it's served is welcome and automatically invited to share it. A young girl brings a small calabash filled with water for everyone in turn to wash their hands, while her mother places a series of steaming bowls in the middle of the yard. The fisherman briefly rinses his paws and makes a beeline for the head of the family. Discussing how bad the catch has been lately, he positions himself cross-legged on a mat and begins to pay tribute to the woman's efforts. Mmm! You can smell the spices in the *talalé*, a dish fit for a king! Our women are the only ones who can make such delicious fish couscous, and that's a fact!

As for Madické, his stomach's in knots. A late lunch is his excuse to decline the invitation politely. Besides, unlike the older generation, he doesn't like sharing other people's meals whenever circumstances dictate. If this match hadn't gone on, he'd have extricated himself before supper-time. While some wolf down mouthfuls of couscous and compliment the cook to justify their greed, he savours the calm created in front of the TV.

'Great,' he says to himself, 'I can watch the penalties in peace.'

But the weather decided otherwise. He'd hardly had this thought when a series of lightning flashes ripped through the sky. A violent tornado whipped the coconut palm branches. The white sand, the islanders' pride, became their worst enemy, a whirlwind flagellating their skin and carrying off everything in its path. The people eating quickly deserted their mats, which were either flung against the fence or swirled above their heads. Then big raindrops began to fall: one of the first June rains, often short-lived but always unpredictable, that let Sahelians know it's the start of the winter season and time to work in the fields.

Madické hadn't waited for the first drops of water to seize the old set and carry it into the living room, but in vain. At the first flash of lightning, the TV had blinked and then, letting out a last beep, had abruptly died. He didn't want to think the worst: that beep wasn't a last sigh; the TV couldn't have given up the ghost. He told himself it was an electrical whim, just a shock, a kind of heart attack brought on by the virulence of the lightning flashes. In the living room he attempted a long, solitary resuscitation, with no success. He needed to hear the owner's verdict to convince him to leave the patient's bedside: 'I think it's dead. There's nothing you can do; it doesn't like the rainy season. Last year, too, it died on me at the first clap of thunder. Luckily I managed to get it going again. This time, I think it's finished.'

With his hand resting on the television, the man smiled as he talked on. Glancing at the living room clock, Madické realised bitterly that the penalty shoot-out was finished, too. He politely stammered some excuses and left.

2

OUTSIDE, THE RAIN HAD REFRESHED the earth; the coconut palms were almost motionless, as after every tornado, their branches strewn on the ground. The sand no longer seeped into sandals; it offered its damp, round back to the tread and might have been thought harmless had it not turned informer: you could easily follow the trail of deep footsteps that led to the call office. As he walked, Madické remembered the television owner's smile. His reaction was delayed: 'His TV's broken and he smiles. What a weirdo. Maybe he was happy to see the back of us at last?'

Perhaps Madické had guessed correctly, but that wasn't the only reason. In fact, the television didn't matter much to the man. Like his black-market Rolex that he didn't know how to set, like his leather living room suite, still encased in cotton covers, like his freezer and his refrigerator, both locked away, like his third wife, eclipsed by the fourth, whom he only noticed when the rota of his conjugal duties obliged him to, that television was there, in his huge house, as a sign of his success.

A native of the island, stuffed with his mother's couscous and indignant at his father's poverty, he'd begun by using his brawn, unloading cargo in Dakar port. This hard labour had in no way altered his determination: poverty is the visible face of hell, it's better to die than stay poor, he used to say. To encourage him, or edge him closer to suicide, his father's tired but unforgettable voice echoed in his mind: *Never forget, every scrap of life must serve to win dignity!*

He'd seen some of his friends return to the village in crates packed with ice – killed by tetanus, an ammonia leak or crushed beneath tonnes of rice – but he'd kept going. Then, one day, his parents had asked the schoolteacher to read aloud a letter that had arrived from France.

'What? Our son's in France!' his mother had exclaimed, as the teacher looked on in amusement.

'*Allah Akbar!* God is great! *Alhamdoulilah!* Thanks be to Allah,' his father had said three times, with slightly more restraint.

Thanks to their son's sporadic money orders, their lives changed, little by little but fast enough for it to be noticed. They were less and less in debt at the grocer's, who now greeted them with big smiles and spent more time making small talk. Every two years, their son came back in the summer for a whole month. He'd distribute a few banknotes and French-made trinkets, which no one would swap for a block of emerald. Here, the cheapest tat from Barbès makes you a somebody, and you can't put a price on that!

At the end of his second holiday, the man from Barbès married the little village girl his parents had chosen for him. She was not their first choice, but he had to make do. His first fiancée hadn't had the patience to wait the two long years he'd spent in France, before he'd announced his second visit home. Her name was Sankèle. Her beauty made the islanders' hairs stand on end and her voice drew tears from fishermen's widows, but she never broke into one of those laments that the women of the island sing to beseech the divinities for the return of their adventuring menfolk. Despite a traditional upbringing that attempted to mould her like shea butter, Sankèle had grown up with the wings of a pelican that longs for the open skies. In spite of her shy smile and elusive eyes, she had courage and daring. She'd inherited her mother's features, but not her vision of the world. She had her own ideas about love. What could you expect from a man on the other side of the world, except a widow's nights and wrinkles by the dozen every time he returns? Guided by her own laws, Sankèle had strayed, her future in-laws cried dishonour, turned their backs on her and decided on a less flirtatious ewe to sacrifice when their prodigal son returned. The boy, although illiterate, had begun to use the French 'r'. He knew this girl wouldn't agree to oral sex right away, but what did that matter, she was from a good family and had all the makings of a submissive wife; in time, he'd be able to shape her as he pleased. For now, he wanted only to prove he'd remained a son who was faithful to tradition. He didn't ask what had become of his first fiancée; he was sure his folks had made the right decision, in full knowledge of the facts. He had no time to lose. His mother was getting old; a young wife around the house would help her and, most important, it's cheaper than a maid. He consoled himself for the sacrifice made to his parents by telling himself that he could marry a woman of his choosing later on, a sophisticated girl who wore make-up. Later, he was sure of it, he'd have the kind who buys lace panties and Yves Saint-Laurent off-the-peg *Made in Taiwan*. When you come from France, you can take your pick, he knew that. And this way no one could boast of knowing what he was up to in France. When he arrived, they were content to admire his spending power, which was astronomical compared with the island average. He at least could afford to replace the eternal rice and fish with a delicious chicken stew.

On his third trip he began to build his impressive residence. The evening the first stone was laid, his father, who'd presided over the blessings, died. Surfeit of happiness? Heart attack? The nurse wasn't there to say. Because they loved him too much to let his soul wander long between two worlds, they buried him quickly before feasting on the succulent funeral meal laid on by his son. His widow began her period of seclusion, and the family observed three days of mourning, punctuated by the weeping women's lamentations and summons to eat. After he'd honoured his father's memory at great cost, the man from Barbès resumed the building works.

Every scrap of life must serve to win dignity!

This house would for ever ensure the villagers' respect and admiration. The structural work was completed when, in Barbès, he sold the various presents the villagers had given him. During his next holiday he finished his house, moved his family from the shack he'd been born in and took a second wife, slightly more modern than the first. She worked as a maid for a bourgeois family in the capital, whose manners and language she imitated. Dripping with sweat in her long damask dresses, her heels buried in the sand, she fluttered her eyelashes and slipped a few French words into her speech. She had just two years to enjoy her privileges as the new chosen one; a third, then a fourth wife came to topple her from the throne.

On his seventh trip, the man from Barbès built a well-stocked shop at the entrance to his house and moved to the village for good. As the symbol of successful emigration, his advice was now sought on every matter; faces turned polite on meeting him, and even the sand softened as his long starched *boubou* swept by. Still wondering how he made his money in France? Listen to the Sonacotra grapevine.

As for Madické, he was asking himself other questions as he reached the call office: what had happened in the penalty shoot-out? Had Maldini taken one? As captain, it was practically certain. Maybe he'd scored? Maybe Italy had won? And why not? Maldini on his own could put the Dutch army to flight.

'Evening, Maldini, you OK? Want to call your sister?' asked the young woman, revealing all the splendour of her teeth.

'Evening, Ndogou,' Madické replied with a start.

Absorbed in his thoughts, he'd stopped automatically without greeting her.

'How are you? No damage, I hope? What with the tornado earlier,' he added, as if to earn her forgiveness.

But the interest he affected to show Ndogou was no mask for his anxiety. His last question was simply a diversion tactic, a shrewd way of gleaning information about the condition of the telephone.

Rising from her chair in the doorway, Ndogou, who'd seen through his question, announced gently: 'Someone's using the phone. As soon as he's finished, you can go in.'

Ndogou, who was considered an intellectual due to a brief spell in high school, occupies an important position in the village. She's responsible for what's known here as the call office: a small room where the one telephone, which serves the whole neighbourhood, rests on its altar. People come with scraps of paper, scribbled with two or three phone numbers, to make their calls in exchange for a few coins. Illiterate for the most part, they often need the young woman's help to dial a number. But Ndogou's work mostly consists in pacing the village from eight a.m. to ten p.m. looking for the villagers wanted on the phone by loved ones on the other side of the world.

'God bless you, my daughter!' called the old man leaving the call office, his beard buried deep in the neck of his kaftan. 'I'll settle up with you soon. My son, the one in Italy, has promised me a money order.'

Old people's prayers are worth more than banknotes, they say here. And what if the angels did a little accounting? In prayer money, how much is a phone call, a loaf of bread, a kilo of rice, a litre of oil, a bar of soap, a pair of shoes or a prescription dictated by malaria?

Ndogou nodded agreement, took out her notebook and added to the long list of outstanding payments. Everyone who runs a business in the village has a notebook like hers. The island's overflowing with old men who can no longer fish or plough their fields – productive in the old days, now reclaimed by forest – and with migrants' wives, surrounded by their broods, who consume on credit, on the strength of a promised money order.

Madické was beginning to hop up and down with impatience. Ndogou gave him a big smile, closed her notebook, reset the counter to zero and uttered the longed-for words: 'Go on, Maldini. I'm sorry, you can't hurry the old ones. Before, they'd wait to be called, but now they've started to come and phone when they haven't even got the—'

Madické didn't hear the rest. He already had the receiver pressed to his ear.

In Strasbourg I was celebrating Italy's win over Holland with a brimming pot of tea, listening to Yandé Codou Sène, the Senegalese Serer diva, and stuffing myself with cakes. Joy at the victory did give me an urge to indulge, but really it was Yandé Codou's voice slowly bewitching me and awakening a melancholy I wanted to suppress at all costs. Certain music, songs or food can suddenly remind you of your state of exile, either because they're too close to your roots or too far from them. In those moments, trying to stay Zen, I'm all in favour of globalisation, because it turns out things with no identity, no soul, too diluted to stir the least emotion in us. Nostalgia is my lot. I have to come to terms with it, keep the music of my homeland in my relic drawer, along with the photos of my loved ones who are for ever buried under Niodior's hot sand.

Comfortably ensconced, I was channel-surfing now, but my attention was soon caught by a particular scene. It featured budding starlets straight out of central casting, a gaggle of airheads with not the faintest idea of the struggles waged for women's dignity. Stealing notes from various composers from the five continents, they screeched their moronic ditties, displaying their anorexic bodies. Good God! Bring back Piaf, Brel, Brassens, Barbara and Gainsbourg, whose songs flow like limpid springs, reaching even the remotest corners of the Sahel. There, a sweet drop of French would fall in your ear, from there to the tip of your tongue, never to leave you. Mmm, their words were good enough to eat.

I was starting on my second box of cakes and my third cup of tea when the phone rang.

'Hello! Yes, it's me. Ring me back at the call office.'

'Madické? You OK?'

'Yes. Ring me back now.'

00221…it's not a number, it's the part of my throat where France Telecom presses the pitiless blade of its knife. France to Senegal: the unit cost is high for students who are farmers' sons, for those domestic goddesses who dress at Tati, for shop security guards who build up their muscles on noodles, tourists who visit Paris huddled on dumper trucks or gardeners who cut roses for Madame Dupont without ever being able to offer one to their luscious wives. I find the rate as indecent as hitting someone who's dying. When Senghor was dreaming up the notion of Francophony, he should have borne in mind that the Frenchman is richer than most of the French-speaking world and negotiated a deal to spare us this communications racket.

Only overwhelming nostalgia, the irresistible plea of a worried mother or impatient brother, can make me dial 00221. I pick up the receiver. It's black. It ought to be red, red with the blood I pour into France Telecom.

'Hello! Madické? Yes, it's me. Is everything OK?'

'Yes, everything's OK. Did you watch the match?'

'Yes, I did. How are Grandpa and Grandma?'

'Fine. Who won? Did you watch the penalty shoot-out?'

'Yes. How are—'

'Everyone's fine! Tell me! Who took the penalties?'

Everyone's fine, that's a bit thin, but I don't press him. I know I won't have any real news before I've delivered my match report.

'Di Biagio lined up first, you should have seen his face. He eyed the ball so intensely he looked like a matador about to take on an angry bull in a Spanish arena. On the terraces, everyone held their breath, then the ball flew off like an arrow and—'

'He scored? Tell me, did he score?'

'Yes, he scored, and—'

'And then, go on, what then?'

'Then it was the Dutch captain's turn, but luckily Toldo took off as if he had wings…'

'Toldo saved the ball. And then?'

'A Dutch player, you know, number—'

'No, just tell me about the Italian players.'

'Pessoto, you could see in his eyes he wanted to set the Dutch goal on fire, quick as a flash—'

'He scored? Did he score?'

'Yes, and so did Totti; he scored the third goal. The Italian banners were waving all over the stadium, the supporters were getting bolder, they—'

'And Maldini? Did Maldini take one?'

'Yes, he took one. A captain worth his salt can't let his

troops go to the front without him. Even if he'd given the right orders, Maldini had to put them into practice himself and prove that—'

'Did he score? Tell me!'

'Well, stop interrupt—'

'Yeah, sorry! So? Did he score?'

'No, he missed!'

'Oh shit! But did we win? Go on, did they win?'

'If you'd let me tell you how the Dutch players got on at the same time, you'd know by now, but you're so impatient that—'

'Come on, did they still win?'

'Yes!'

'By how many goals? What was the score? Please!'

'Three–one.'

'Great! I knew they'd win! Fantastic! Right, I've got to go. They'll be waiting for me at home. Me and the boys have organised a dance for tonight.'

'Wait. How's Grandma? Is she well?'

'Yes. Don't forget to watch the final, France–Italy. It's on the second of July at six p.m. in Senegal. With the time difference, that means eight p.m. in France. Bye.'

'Hey, that's not the only bloody thing in my life!' I yelled, but there was only a beep by way of reply. 'Goodbye, you little twit,' I murmured before dropping the receiver.

It's always the same scenario. He makes me call him and I bankrupt myself reporting football matches, but it's impossible to drag any news out of him. Football's all he thinks about! One day I'll stuff my phone bill in his mouth to teach him to listen to me.

Still, I'm happy I've heard Madické's voice. I know that he's well, at least; and if the family had a serious problem he'd have told me. Men don't like details, they say, and he, even as a kid, had it drummed into him that he must behave like a man. He's been taught to say 'Ow!', to grit his teeth, not to cry when he's hurt or afraid. As a reward for the courage he had to show in all circumstances, a throne had been built for him high above the female sex. A male, then, and proud of it, this true *guelwaar* has enjoyed a princely dominance since childhood: beneficiary of his father's rare smiles, the biggest bit of fish, the best of his mother's doughnuts and the last word when women are present.

I replace the receiver. I'm only a moderate feminist but, really, that's going too far. I'm could get get depressed. I stretch out on the sofa and start up a conversation with my hormones. They're not always helpful: not only do they make me suffer at that time of the month, but it's their fault I'm silenced. Without my say-so, they've been named 'submission'; I don't like that word, with its three s's, those conspiratorial constrictives that suppress love and admit only the breath of authoritarianism. I don't like sub-missions; I prefer real missions. And I love high heels, too. Will Marie Curie be wearing them at the gatherings with the great and the good? I have no idea. On the other hand, I'm sure all the great men of this world have knelt down, at least once in their lives, to kiss the foot of a woman wearing them. So I'm keeping my female hormones! I wouldn't want testicles for the world. Besides, some men rip them off so they can strut around the Bois de Boulogne in their high heels, parading their hairy chests.

I stand up and put on some rousing music. Youssou N'Dour says what he likes, the drummer sends me into a trance and I dance. Hands on knees, I shake my arse: the fan dance, the one Senegalese women excel at, the one that has men's tongues hanging down to their knees wherever it's danced, rocking the fragile throne of virility, making even the toughest macho forget his own father's name, suddenly ready to grovel for the privilege of counting the beads round a sensuous beauty's waist till the end of the night. She, however, will be the one who decides, with a mocking smile, when they will have sex. The next morning, to wash her little, suggestively embroidered *pagne*, she'll open her hand (clenched since her orgasm) and a butterfly will fly out, which, outside, reckons it's an elephant. Maybe that's why my grandma told me that in the secrecy of the home, an elephant becomes as light as a butterfly. Madame can tame wild beasts, but outside she'll go all submissive and fragile. Please, sir, help me: a spider! Help, get it out of here. I'm so scared of spiders! Oh thank you, kind gentlemen. What would we do without you?

Tired of dancing, I settle down with a bottle of water and turn on the television again. The late news is beginning, giving the match score and commenting: 'France–Italy. What a line-up for the European Cup Final!' There'll be a scramble for tickets, if they're not all sold already. Apparently some touts have been arrested for selling them for exorbitant sums on the black market. Then they replay the images from the end of the last match. Maldini makes a brief appearance. Ha! Him again! I swear he won't leave me alone. I channel-surf: a whole evening's programming devoted to inveterate gamblers, people who travel the globe in search of casinos. But what planet are we living on? We're surrounded by crackpots, and my brother's one of them. If he could travel the world to see Maldini's matches, he would, I know he would.

Don't forget to watch the final on the second of July. And I wait. Who could still dare say distance brings freedom? That little sentence was enough to plunge me into a state of antici-pation and put the rest of my life on hold. But, for Madické, what in my life in France could be more important than that match? In paradise, you don't struggle, you don't fall ill, you don't ask questions: it's enough to be alive, you can afford everything you desire, including the luxury of time, and that automatically means you're available. That's how Madické imagined my life in France. He'd seen me leave on the arm of a Frenchman after a lavish wedding which gave no hint of the storms to come. Even when he was told of them, he couldn't know what the consequences would be. Setting off with masks, statues, dyed cotton fabrics and a stripey ginger cat, I'd arrived in France in my husband's luggage just as if I'd landed with him in the Siberian tundra. But once in his country, my skin cast a shadow over the idyll – his family wanting only Snow White – the festivities were short-lived and the trouble enduring. Alone, surrounded by my masks instead of the seven dwarfs, determined not to return home in shame after a failure that many had gleefully predicted, I stubbornly went on with my studies. It was no use telling Madické that as a cleaning woman my survival depended on the number of floor cloths I got through. He persisted in imagining I wanted for nothing, living like royalty at the court of Louis XIV. Accustomed to going without in his underdeveloped country, he wasn't going to feel sorry for a sister living in one of the world's great powers after all! He couldn't help his illusions. The third world can't see Europe's wounds, it is blinded by its own; it can't hear Europe's cry, it is deafened by its own. Having someone to blame lessens your suffering, and if the third world started to see the west's misery, it would lose the target of its anger. For Madické, living in a developed country was in itself a huge advantage I had over him, he with the family and the tropical sun. How could I have made him understand the loneliness of exile, my fight for survival and the permanent effort my studies demanded? Wasn't I the layabout who'd chosen the European Eden, playing the eternal schoolgirl at an age when most of my childhood friends were cultivating their plot of land and feeding their offspring? Absent and useless to them in their daily lives, what was the point of me, unless it was occasionally to decant a little of the nectar they imagined was slaking my thirst in France? Blood often forgets its duties, but never its rights. It dictated its law to me. Having chosen a path that was completely foreign to my people, I was determined to prove its value to them. I had to 'succeed' so as to take on the job assigned every child from our country: to be the family's social security. This obligation to help is the migrant's heaviest burden. But, since what we most prize remains the love and recognition of those we've left behind, their slightest whim becomes an order. *Don't forget to watch the final on the second of July.* From that moment on, I felt I'd been invested with a sacred mission. My attention was hijacked; only memories linked with Madické and his world had any claim on me.

3

MY BROTHER'S PASSION FOR FOOTBALL started early. When he was a child, our mother gave him a rubber ball she'd bought in town. He learned to walk and to kick it at the same time. When he fell over, he'd crawl towards the ball, stand up and kick it, before falling over again. Our mother would encourage him with praise: 'Bravo, my son. You're a champion!'

Even more determined, he'd repeat the whole performance. With the years, his steps became steadier, his shots more precise, and kicking the round ball on his own began to lose its appeal. At Koranic school, he'd wait impatiently for break time to play with his friends. In spite of the lectures of the schoolteacher, who disapproved of football, the game continued after classes. A real ball was rare. Resourceful, like all third-world kids, the boys would collect rags or sponges and roll them into a ball in a plastic bag to enable them to pursue their passion. The type of ball might vary from one week to the next, the rules of the game might be stretched from time to time – sometimes techniques closer to traditional wrestling broke out on the pitch – but practising their favourite sport was like a calling and nothing could stop it for long. No one could prevent them racing to those waste grounds from which they'd return exhausted, covered in dust, their feet full of splinters.

For a long time their only role models were the older children who went to the French primary school. They were organised in teams and coached by the teacher, calling themselves by the names of their French idols on the pitch. The rare African-sounding names belonged to the few home-grown kids who played overseas, mostly in France. So, every Saturday afternoon, Captain Michel Platini and company would kick up the dust of Niodior to the great delight of their small, always adoring fans. The kids would never miss the weekly match. But one Saturday – it was well before I left for France – Platini and his team-mates played without the usual clamour to boost them. The small sand-dunes that lined the pitch, still bumpy from the onslaught of last week's crowd, witnessed the match in silence. Only the teacher's whistle punctuated moves that previously triggered the applause and praise of a devoted public. The match was tougher than usual. Discouraged, the players felt the sand swallow their feet up to the ankle and their movements become increasingly sluggish. Wretched is he who reads his glory in the public's fickle gaze! When the final whistle blew, frizzy-haired Captain Platini and his sidekicks still had no idea that a great event had just turned the island's life upside down.

The village had received its first television! The man from Barbès, who'd arrived the night before, had waited until mid-afternoon, just before normal kickoff time, to unpack his bags. From one of his magical suitcases he'd produced this astonishing device, to the wide-eyed stares of his four wives, flanked by toddlers he knew only by name. The news spread like wildfire, and the village kids didn't need to be told twice. For the first time in their lives, the majority of the villagers could try out this strange thing they'd already heard about: they could see whites speaking, singing, dancing, eating, kissing, fighting – see whites, in fact, really living, there in the box, just behind the glass. The spectacle went on late into the night. How amazed they were when they saw one of their countrymen report news about this country and abroad, with pictures and everything! So blacks could use whites' magic, too! The only disappointment, for there was one, was the impossibility of understanding what the journalist was on about, despite his hand signals. Questioning looks assailed Ndogou; expelled from school for constantly failing her exams, she'd returned to the village and wasn't yet working at the call office, which didn't exist then. So she acted as translator: 'The presidential plane took off from Dakar international airport this morning at eight a.m. Today, the nation's father, accompanied by our honorable Minister for Development, is in Tambacounda unveiling a water pump given by our friends the Japanese. At the end of the day, his Excellency the Prime Minister went to the autonomous port of Dakar to take delivery of a cargo of rice donated by France in order to help the drought-stricken people of the interior. France, a great country and our long-time friend, has conveyed through its Minister for Foreign Affairs that it is preparing to reassess Senegal's debt in the near future. Health now: our Minister for Health has highlighted a clear upsurge in malaria cases with the arrival of the first rains. Teams of trainee doctors, familiarly called bush doctors, will soon be sent into rural areas. Finally, to end this news bulletin, I'm delighted to tell you that our valiant national sportsmen in France are distinguishing themselves in the French club league, as shown by these images from our colleagues at France 2. According to the Minister for Youth and Sports, they should soon be back home to train with the other players in the national team, in the run-up to the African Nations' Cup. Ladies and gentlemen, good night.'

The interpreter had no need to translate this last sentence: everyone managed a loud 'good night', and an old woman even waved at the journalist, whose image lingered for a moment, distorted and shaky. Of course, it was more than thirty years since Jean Frémont[1] had built his television, but *our* cameramen were still at the teething stage. As yet the image was as capricious as it was mysterious.

Madické and his friends were in raptures over the beautiful stadiums and the brief report; a few quick sequences, a rapid summary of the previous day's French matches: a Senegalese player had scored a goal, after making mincemeat of the big fair-haired player attempting to put him off his game.

The adults did not react. They preferred wrestling to football and didn't feel especially concerned by the news they'd just heard. Here, there's no need for a water pump, even a Japanese one. Lying out in the Atlantic, the island of Niodior has seemingly inexhaustible ground water; a small number of wells supplies the whole village. You need only dig four or five metres to see a spurt of fresh, clear spring water, filtered by the fine-grained sand. Nor is anyone dependent on a few kilos of French rice; these islanders – growers, breeders and fishermen – are all self-sufficient and ask nothing of anyone. If they'd wanted, they could have set up a mini-republic within the Senegalese Republic and the government wouldn't have cottoned on for years, until the elections came around. Anyway, they're forgotten on all counts, the dispensary's almost bare; they rely on herbal infusions for curing malaria. The nation's father, our President, can offer his paternity if he likes, but here no one expects a thing from his protection. In other words, they couldn't care less about the government or what the newscaster had to say about it.

In a few weeks everyone had an idea of the television programmes and came to watch the ones that interested them. Nights passed, bolstered by the bluish glow from the small screen. Seasons flowed by in the sound. One year followed the next, shortening the time granted the living and lengthening the muscles of the young footballers. The faithful Atlantic still sucked at the beautiful island's feet, but the local Platini and his team-mates no longer had a crowd to watch them. In the hearts of their young fans, they'd been replaced by the players seen on TV. Little by little, football fever had taken hold of all the kids in the village. They formed teams named after their favourite clubs and stayed faithful to them throughout their youth, each boy taking the name of his hero. So, on the sandy pitches, marked out by four hastily gathered wooden sticks for goal posts, you could watch Paris-St-Germain take on Marseilles, or Nantes crush Lens, if it wasn't Sochaux struggling against Strasbourg.

The television showed other big European clubs, too, but there was nothing doing. After the historically recognised colonisation, a kind of mental colonisation now prevails: the young players worshipped and still worship France. In their eyes, everything desirable comes from France.

Hence, even the television that allows them to see matches comes from France. Its owner, now an important man in the village, lived in France. The schoolteacher, a knowledgeable man, did part of his training in France. All those with important jobs in the country have studied in France. The wives of our successive presidents are all French. To win the elections, the nation's father first wins over France. The few rich and famous Senegalese footballers play in France. To train the national team, they always seek out a Frenchman. Even our ex-President awarded himself retirement in France, so he would live longer. Thus, on the island, even if we can't tell France from Peru on a map, we're well aware it rhymes with chance.

Only Madické had departed from the rules and gone for an Italian team, AC Milan. Since he was in the minority, he'd agreed to play alongside his childhood friends in a team with a thoroughly French name. But because he always attempted to copy the moves and body language of the AC Milan skipper, his friends called him Maldini, to tease him. Far from being insulted, he was honoured, and his whole life revolved around his new identity. From simple fan, he'd been promoted to the level of clone. He only ever wore Maldini's number and played in the same position as him. Between sowing and harvest, Maldini shirts replaced the greater part of his wardrobe; even off the pitch, you could tell him by his shirt. Though he and his friends shared a passion for football, when it came to a match between Italy and France he felt isolated from the group. In this relentlessly Francophile universe, his match forecasts were never welcome. So he'd learned to keep them to himself, even when Italy was playing another country. When that happened, only the old fisherman would bother him for conversation. Madické wasn't keen on these discussions, or rather he was tired of them, because there was always a hidden agenda.

The old man always wanted exact information on different matches. Stuck to him like a leech, he'd let him go only after a detailed report. Unlike the boys who openly bragged about their favourite teams, the old man, just like Madické, kept his bets to himself. His fishing sometimes made him miss important matches on the television, so he'd got into the habit of asking Madické for the results, but never those relating to a particular team. He'd find out about Sochaux, Strasbourg, Nancy, Nantes, Marseilles, and so on. He was happy when the team he'd asked about had lost, and sad when it had won. My brother no longer knew what to expect from this grilling. He was a fan of Maldini, of AC Milan, not of all the French clubs! He was sick of answering so many questions from such a disloyal supporter. It was already puzzling that, instead of joining his own generation under the palaver tree, this fellow should presume familiarity with the boys to talk football, but even more bizarre that he behaved like a weathercock.

'So which team do you support?' Madické had finally asked.

'Oh, I like them all,' the old fisherman muttered. 'I love the beautiful game.'

'Yes, but there must be one team you think plays better than the others, isn't there?'

'No, it varies. Life would be boring if genius didn't do the rounds, if talent became exclusive...'

Madické had understood: that kind of comment was the dam old people built to divert impetuous streams of questions. Just as a snail whose flesh is prodded shrinks back into its shell, the old man had taken refuge behind the mystery of words. After four friendly pats which meant *I have you fooled*, he said goodbye to his young friend, carrying off the secret he imagined inviolable. But he'd reckoned without Madické's perspicacity and the gossip he picked up. On the island, nothing is really said; news is drawn with water from the well, and the whole village drinks from the same spring. Family stories, even the most ancient, float in the women's pots, and they serve them up with their own sauce later on. Don't think for a moment that their cooking stinks! It's just the Atlantic Ocean discharging its filth on the island's shores! If you listen hard, you might hear the old fisherman's story in the sound of the waves.

In his youth, he'd been handsome and vigorous. A well-known wrestler, he'd take part in tournaments up and down the country, which he'd often win. Famous and much in demand, it was rumoured he loved the pleasures of the flesh. Countless women were ready and willing to satisfy his champion's appetite, so naturally his conquests mounted up. Generously, he wished to honour those he felt were worthy, and almost all of them were, since lesser beauties didn't dare join the parades that formed on his arrival. At the peak of his career, one of his tournaments resulted in the birth of a magnificent boy. A little over nine months after his return, the young mother, accompanied by her parents, came to the village to present his son to him. He unceremoniously denied paternity; blinded by his fame, he didn't want to burden himself with a family and call a stop while the going was so good. His parents supported his decision: their son couldn't marry a young woman who offered her charms to a passing lover. Covered in shame, the poor girl, who was hoping to marry a champion, returned with her parents as discreetly as she'd come. As an unmarried mother, she was denigrated, then banished from the community, and finally exiled herself with her son to the city. Some said she worked as a maid; others imagined a less respectable activity. But in the desert you can always happen on an oasis. As she was beautiful and quick-witted, a city dweller succumbed to her charms and put an end to her ordeal. He was a lot older than her, but she didn't mind the age difference. A rich trader with no children, he was delighted to take in mother and son and to act as father. He who takes the hen accepts the chicks! She married him but wanted her son to keep his real father's name. Her husband, a little offended at this curtailment of his rights, nevertheless did all he could for the child's education and made him his heir. Later, the boy, who played football in the Dakar team, was taken on by a French club. In no time he'd become one of the most famous Senegalese overseas players. Reporters, fascinated by his game and his playboy looks, shouted out his name at matches. Rich and famous, he was a hero back home. The disgraced child was now received by the head of state. *Allah Akbar!* Meanwhile, at the end of his wrestling career, the old fisherman had married a suitable young local woman, with whom he had one daughter.

Madické was pondering many questions, but he felt confused when he saw his old friend: why wouldn't the old boy have a favourite team like any other supporter? Perhaps he did have one, but which? Finding no answer to the riddle, he carried out a cross-check. What did all the teams he asked about have in common? Suddenly the penny dropped: one after the other, they'd all played against the same French club, the one the famous Senegalese played for! This and the rumours that were rife on the island convinced him he was on to something: the man was secretly following his son's career! He *did* support a team but was determined not to say, out of embarrassment or for fear of confirming the gossip, letting it be known that he regretted abandoning his only son. Acting the sleuth, Madické could now tell in advance which matches would interest the old man, but he went on as if nothing had changed. The game continued as before: the old boy still asked his questions with the same detachment and Madické answered them, feigning innocence.

A secret is like milk on the fire: it will boil over if you don't watch out. There's a limit to every deception; it's not easy to pretend not to know what you know. Madické was well brought up; he had no intention of unmasking the old man. But milk on the fire, passion in the heart, pressure of an event, excitement – and the milk boils over. Should he clear up the mess? Madické could keep it in no longer; unhappily, words have no bodies or you could grab on to them to hold them back. So the words swelled with emotion, undulated, stretched, spun and then exploded in the fisherman's astonished face: 'They slaughtered Bordeaux three–nil!' Madické yelled, instantly putting his hand over his mouth.

The old fisherman, who'd just drawn level with him, looked suddenly seasick; in his eyes could be read: *What does he mean, they? Shit, the boy's rumbled me!* He reeled slightly, but composed himself quickly enough to change the subject: 'One of these days you'll be going to France to play football, too,' he declared, looking his young friend straight in the eye.

Boats often pitch, but they don't necessarily take in water. To pitch is not to capsize, they say here. Madické may not have been aware of it, but the old fisherman was a good sailor and knew how to ride the right wave. The look on the young man's face was only a question mark. He should savour the moment; his verbal assault would bear its fruit. After thoroughly enjoying his first strike, the old boy elaborated: 'Well, now, isn't that the reason you spend time with the foreigner? I've seen you in the team the school-teacher coaches. Apparently he's teaching you whites' language now. You're doing your utmost to get out, aren't you? Isn't that so? Well, I know you'll be going to play football in France one day. I've seen it in the cowries.'

I'd been living in France for some years by then. Like everyone in the village, the old man knew all about it. My first holidays, alone, hadn't gone unnoticed. I'd come without the white man they'd rejected initially, and then had to accept, since they had no hold over me. So many of them took an interest in my relationship, hoping their spiteful predictions would come true. When I arrived, even people I hadn't known before came to visit me and pronounce on my new life. Despite their thinly disguised satisfaction, they criticised me for my divorce. 'A donkey never leaves good hay,' the men would say as I passed: if a man leaves his wife, it's because she hasn't been a good wife. Nosy gossips came to see me and prayed for my fertility. 'The farmer,' they'd say, 'expects a harvest from his seeds.' I said nothing, so they'd use their many household chores as excuses to make way for another group. Making themselves at home without my say-so, the newcomers would exchange glances, then an attempt at a maternal voice would clog my ears: 'A woman's honour is in her milk.' Their pendulous breasts attested to their respect for this age-old adage. What mouth would have dared mention the pill in front of them, at the risk of being cursed for life? Telling them that in Europe, women could control the number of children they had would have been taken as provocation. Aware how pointless it was to try to explain, I put up with them in silence, with the polite patience tradition required of me. After a few visits, the ingenuity with which they interfered in my life no longer shocked me. I envied their serenity, the psychological comfort they doubtless derived from the strength of their convictions. They seemed to have solved all the equations I found so mysterious. They were menhirs of tradition, untouched by the whirlwind of cultural intermixing that made me waver. They followed their path. I was searching for mine in the opposite direction; we had nothing to say to each other. Solemn-faced, they'd set off again, full of their unanswered questions, diagnosing sterility, the main cause of divorce in the village.

Despite the whispering, they'd lower themselves to extract money or a T-shirt from me in the name of a custom – one that prevents many poorer migrants coming home for the holidays – which has it that the returning migrant must bring presents, presents whose value is calculated by how far you've come and your relation to the recipient. In spite of myself I went along with their excessive expectations of people 'from France'. My family and friends suffered on account of their greed: as soon as I arrived, it was thought they had a fortune at their disposal. When I had nothing left to give, they'd let themselves be stripped of the little they'd received, just to save face. Wild plans were devised concerning them. Some said I was going to take my brother with me, others that I'd arrange for him to come to France later. I'd left without comment. When the old fisherman spoke to Madické about going to France in the future, had he really seen it in the cowries or was he simply joining in the calculation of probabilities practised by most of the villagers?

I don't know what the fisherman had really seen in his cowries. On the other hand, I knew how much Madické's growing passion had cost me, in the time I'd been living in France. As well as the hours spent watching matches that weren't always thrilling, I raced through sports shops, my brother's kit list in my hand. The telephone was no longer just a tube through which France Telecom sucked my blood; it had become a cudgel. The requests rolled in, not spelled out but cleverly insinuated and irresistible: a pair of boots for training, another with studs for matches, shin pads, a leather ball, a cup for an inter-island club championship and, of course, a Maldini shirt. I found them all, apart from the shirt – I've never been fond of cult objects.

My brother played in the village team now and the matches became more and more important. His talents were maturing under the schoolteacher's watchful eye. But their relationship didn't stop there. Madické had realised that everyone who went to play overseas spoke French – not the best, but French all the same. So he asked for evening classes with the schoolteacher. The curiosities of local life held no more attractions for this city man; the discreet rustle of the coconut palm branches was no longer enough to chase away the immense sadness in his heart. Dusk would bring a procession of memories that made his eyes fill with tears. A lesson at that time of day, far from being a chore, would be a welcome distraction for him. In any case, teaching was his vocation: 'The seed of knowledge must be sown wherever it's likely to grow,' he'd say. And this was what he did; he'd come from his city to plant his seed in the island's salty sand. The soul of Godot in him was waiting patiently for shoots. To the children he was 'Monsieur Ndétare'. The others merely respected his civil-servant status, but deep down he was just 'the foreigner'. As a favour, or to relieve his solitude, Ndétare agreed to teach Madické, who was speedily building a career plan solely on the strength of future proficiency in the French language.

'Hey, guess what?' he shouted down the telephone one day. 'I've started French lessons with the schoolteacher! You know, your old teacher, Monsieur Ndétare. He said he'd give me evening classes. Do you realise what that means I could do? Maybe I...Well, anyway. Monsieur Ndétare agrees, he's so great. So, you're not saying anything. Don't you remember him?'

4

OF COURSE I REMEMBER HIM.

Monsieur Ndétare, the teacher, already getting on in years. With a blade for a face, forks for hands and legs like stilts to take him to the remotest parts of the country to carry out the work of a devoted civil servant, in places where the state is a mere bystander. Ndétare is distinguishable from the other inhabitants of the island by his silhouette, his ways, his urban manners, his European clothes, his academic French and his complete faith in Karl Marx, whose work he can recite chapter and verse. A trade unionist, he's been head of the village primary school for nearly a quarter of a century, ever since the government, considering him a dangerous agitator, sent him to the island with the mission to teach the children of the proletariat.

Of course I remember him.

I owe him Descartes, I owe him Montesquieu, I owe him Victor Hugo, I owe him Molière, I owe him Balzac, I owe him Marx, I owe him Dostoevsky, I owe him Hemingway, I owe him Léopold Sédar Senghor, I owe him Aimé Césaire, I owe him Simone de Beauvoir, Marguerite Yourcenar, Mariama Bâ and the rest. I owe him my first secretly written love poem, I owe him the first French song I murmured, because I owe him my first phoneme, my first moneme, the first French phrase I read, heard and understood. I owe him my first letter of French, written wonkily on my broken slate. I owe him school. I owe him education. I owe him, in short, my *ambiguous adventure*. Because I pestered him endlessly, he gave me everything: letters, numbers, the keys to the world. And because he fulfilled my first conscious desire, to go to school, I owe him all my small French cancan steps towards the light.

Monsieur Ndétare's classroom was never closed. But I had no right to enter it, I hadn't been enrolled. I was curious, especially intrigued by the words his students uttered when they came out of class – their melodious songs that weren't those of my language, but from another that sounded just as sweet. I wanted to discover the genius who taught the school-children all these mysterious words. So I cheated, I stole, I lied. I betrayed the person I love most in the world, my grandmother. Forgive me, God, forgive me, but it was in a good cause, or I'd never have been able to read Your name in all the holy books. Thank you!

I cheated: my grandparents' house was opposite the primary school. When I went into the garden with my grandmother, I'd dutifully help her water her plants, then I'd wait until she was busy tending her tomatoes, cauliflowers, onions and other vegetables. Pretending to go and rest under the coconut palm at the entrance to the garden, I'd sneak off. I'd dig out the broken slate I'd found in a dustbin and my chalks – I hid them all in a ditch in front of the garden – then I'd slip away to school.

I stole. To buy chalk, I only had to steal a few small coins from my grandmother. She always put her little hand-stitched cotton purse under her pillow.

I lied. When I came home, hours later, I'd make up a story with glaring inconsistencies, and the poor woman would repeat her lecture, which I'd heard too often for it to bother me: 'So there you are! Next time you slip off, tell me, ok? Understood? If you do it again, you'll be sorry. All right?'

At school, as I've already said, Monsieur Ndétare's classroom was never closed. I'd go in. There was an empty desk at the back. I'd sit there, quietly, and listen. He'd be writing strange letters or numbers on the blackboard and instruct the class to copy them. I copied. Then came the moment when he'd call the schoolchildren to the blackboard in turn; when they'd all gone up, I decided I'd go too. Monsieur Ndétare would be annoyed, he'd open the giant compass of his legs and come towards me: 'Off with you, right now! Go on, outside. You're not a member of this class!'

I ran out. As soon as he was behind his desk again, I'd return and take my place in the back row. It was still the era of teaching by radio: the teacher had to make the pupils repeat words and sentences spoken by a voice on a radio cassette player. As soon as everyone had finished, I'd pipe up and repeat them, too, and the circus would begin again. Unable to take any more, Monsieur Ndétare added my name in pencil to the bottom of his official list and from then on decided to have me do all the exercises like the other kids. He no longer sent me away; on the contrary, he gave me extra attention. Seeing that I was doing well, he took me by the hand one day.

'Come on, we're going to see your grandmother.'

'No, no! I don't want to, I can't! She doesn't know I'm coming here! Let me go! Let me go!'

'Well, she's going to know today!'

She'd just come in from the garden. Sitting on a bench, she was emptying her basket of vegetables.

'What have you done now? I've been looking for you everywhere. Where were you?'

'At school,' Monsieur Ndétare replied.

'For goodness' sake, when are you going to do what I say?

How many times do I have to tell you? That school is no place for you!'

'That's exactly what I've come to talk to you about, Madame Sarr.'

'Yes, I know. She won't listen. This time I promise you she won't be bothering you again.'

'No, no, I didn't come for that. I think you ought to let her go. I came to ask for her birth certificate so I can register her, if you don't object.'

She looked at me, utterly stupefied. Here, no one trusts civil servants. You never know what they might report back in high places. It wouldn't occur to anyone to argue with a schoolteacher, a representative of the state, especially at that time when the government was encouraging mass education. Ndétare knew he must strike while the iron was hot.

'She's doing very well, you know, and it would be better for her, too. It won't be long before illiterate people will be unable to get on in this country without help. You must admit it's difficult having to ask someone to write your letters, fill in your forms, or come with you to offices for every little formality. And she's so obstinate she might even pass her primary school certificate.'

After a moment's silence, the matriarch uttered her verdict:

'Well, all right, then. At least later, when she goes to the city on her own, she'll be able to recognise bus numbers and read the street names. Ndakarou, our capital, has turned into a city of *toubabs*. It will stop her getting lost, as I sometimes do.'

This thought found no resonance in my head. To my mind, it was a matter of course that this woman who taught me everything about life could read and write. Our deepest-held convictions, wherever they come from, will always be more poetic, stronger and more reassuring than reality.

She went off to her room, opened a suitcase and returned with a bundle of papers that she held out to the school-teacher. After going through them carefully, he stopped, looking puzzled.

'You have two granddaughters with the same name?'

'No. Why?'

'I found two certificates with the same name, the same year, but a different month. Was it March or June the little one was born?'

'She was born in the month of the first rains, just at the beginning of the winter season, the year the students wrecked the capital.'

Monsieur Ndétare smiled and politely said goodbye.

I continued to sit in on lessons, without being officially enrolled. At the start of the next school year, a father about to enrol his own daughter agreed with the teacher's view and helped my grandmother sort out the papers for school. They settled on the month of the first rains.

Little by little, my grandmother became enthusiastic about my studying. I still thought she could read and write, she kept such a strict watch over my evening revision by the light of the hurricane lamp. Resting my elbows on the table in the living room, I'd read my lessons out loud, then close my eyes and try to recite them. At the first hint of hesitation, her orders were firm: 'Read it again, several times, then repeat it better!'

So I'd start over, again and again, until she was satisfied my reading and reciting had the proper flow. Our evenings were enlivened by this little game for a long time. One day, coming back from school, I ran up to her, my school essay book opened at the right page: 'Look, mama! My essay result!'

She glanced at it and, out of the blue, gave me a slap.

'But why are you slapping me? I came top of the class and

that's not good enough?'

'Stop lying!' she shouted, 'I saw, there's red everywhere. That means a bad mark!'

I went back to school to find Monsieur Ndétare, who was busy tidying his living quarters next to the school. He came with me and explained my results to my grandmother, singing my praises. No doubt regretting the unjust punishment she'd just meted out, she stared at the ground and almost begged: 'Oh, you two, stop bothering me with your school stories! I don't understand any of it. I can't read or write, so leave me alone.'

Her face was sad. I started to cry. I wanted to go on sharing my school stories with her, which were my whole story. 'Those with a good guide don't get lost in the jungle' she'd told me one day, and ever since I wanted only her as companion. I wanted to tread in her footsteps. She had opened the door to the world for me and hummed my first lullaby.

It was right at the beginning of the winter season, she always loved to tell me. A sun as suffocating as morality, weary of torturing human beings, was sinking rapidly into the Atlantic. Heavy clouds brewed the sorrow of a sky that could no longer hold back its tears. The rain was about to fall; nostrils already inhaled its odour. In hurriedly filled-in holes, seeds of hope waited to sprout, to make the earth smile. The granaries were almost empty, and men stayed longer at sea to stave off hunger and avoid the children's tears and their wives' plaintive looks. Between sowing and harvest, fishing was killing for survival, more than ever. That day, while wives fought over the fishermen's catch on the seashore, my grandmother was busily grinding medicinal plants in the back yard of the house, which was surprisingly silent. Her worried eyes stirred the old pot in which she was boiling roots she'd gone to gather at dawn, deep in the forest.

She was sifting other dried, ground roots when a plangent voice made her start – yet she'd been expecting it for days now. She ran to her room to pick up a pile of cotton fabric which she used to cover the floor of the little yard that served as bathroom.

Far away, the wolves' first yowling drew prayers from shepherds and sent calves running back to their mothers' sides. A torch passed from one hand to another. In the yard, the mother handed her daughter the key to the greatest mystery of all. At the same time, the daughter reached the age of her mother, whose generosity and courage she finally realised. The ordeal of birth eradicates the generation gap between women, they say on the island, and it's only after crossing this threshold that girls truly respect their mothers.

In the yard, the breath from the coconut palms could no longer dry the sweat that drenched the young woman squatting on the white cotton. My grandmother made her drink cup after cup of the steaming herbal infusion. Shafts of light from the sky's one red eye fell on the Atlantic, ordering it to deliver to the world the secret hidden in its belly. The first shadows of night thickened the hair of the coconut palms and ran alongside the fencing, when a cry rang out. The only midwife in the village was away; unpredictable as ever, I'd chosen that moment to be born. My grandmother put her faith in her own experience, her plants and her shea butter; she'd had a midwife only for her youngest.

The island had slipped into dusk's black robes and the rain was falling heavily when my grandmother plunged me in the basin containing a herbal bath. 'Born in the rain,' she'd murmured, 'you'll never be afraid when they spit as you go by. The dolphin's baby has no fear of drowning; but you'll have to face the daylight, too.' While I lay enthroned on my white cotton bed, my roots grew over the world's filth, without my knowing: diluting my mother's blood and the streams of my bath, the rainwater filtered down through the soil, to where the Atlantic becomes an invigorating spring. That night, my grandmother watched over her daughter and her illegitimate baby. The pitiless sun melted the cover of night and exposed us to the eyes of morality. Betrayed by my grandmother, tradition – which demanded I be suffocated and a stillborn child announced to the community – married off my mother to a cousin who had always had his eye on her. If they couldn't be rid of me, the guardians of morality wished me to bear the name of the man forced on my mother. My grandmother was firmly against it: 'She will have her real father's name, she's not some bit of seaweed picked up on the beach, she doesn't have water running in her veins but blood, and that blood carries its own name,' she'd repeat obstinately to the numerous delegations that pestered her. The husband of convenience was offended by this refusal, but only outwardly, for he already had a fertile wife at home and wasn't eager to be saddled with another man's child. By taking my mother as a second wife, he wanted to catch up with his friends, boost his virility and multiply his own heirs, without having to shell out for a bride, seeing as she was an unmarried mother.

The barricades had transformed Paris and now spread through the Dakar streets; young people howled their revolt. John Lennon hadn't yet imagined another world. In Niodior it was the depth of the winter season, and it wasn't rain alone that streamed down the cheeks of my mother, who hid her suffering. Each time she locked up her heart, my stepfather would throw me out, alone or with her, in all weathers. When she went at dawn to cut wood or draw water from the well, he'd wrap me in a cloth and leave me in the yard among the puddles. Sometimes my mother would find me covered in dust from the sandstorms. I was for ever contracting bronchitis and conjunctivitis. My stepfather took advantage of my frequent illnesses to rid himself of the incarnation of sin, the devil's daughter – that's what he called me. A neighbour had advised my mother to keep me with her always, on her back. She was unhappy and didn't seem overanxious to protect me. The neighbour grew more and more worried and at last alerted my grandmother, who one night came and stood outside her son-in-law's house. It was late when she spied her daughter wandering around crying, with me on her back. Determined to save me, my grandmother took me away with her. To cure me, she made endless root broths and massaged me with shea butter. As it hadn't been so long since she'd weaned her youngest, she began to breast-feed again; her milk returned in abundance and soon made a tubby baby of me, full of energy. Because love cannot be measured, my grandmother breastfed me without setting a limit, until the day when, past the age of three, I myself no longer asked for the breast. My mother, meanwhile, had just given birth to a boy, Madické, whom she considered her first-born. So, *mater*? My grandmother, mother of perpetual maternity: *madre*, mother, *mamma mia*, *yaye boye*, *nenam*, *nakony*, beloved mama, my mammy-mummy, my real mother!

With those soft hands that cut my umbilical cord and stroked my head – when, as a baby, I sucked the sap from her breast and fell asleep, replete – my grandmother never ceased spinning the thread that bound me to life.

What do they imagine they're teaching me when they explain that $E=mc^2$, since I've been testing the theory of relativity all my life, which is entirely related to that female *guelwaar* whose almond eyes opened a path for me through the shadows of tradition? What does it matter if she can't read or write? None of my paths can light up without her smile.

It was the exactly the same with school. We navigated

together; she wasn't about to abandon ship. After the essay book incident, she went on filling the oil lamp assiduously and sat silently while I did my revision. She'd question Ndétare, whom she now treated like a son, about my results. The schoolteacher shunned neither this human warmth, nor the eggs and vegetables mammy-mummy heaped on him every time she came for information. Perhaps this was her way of repaying him, or maybe she'd taken pity on this poor exiled man, who must have reminded her of one of her sons, then in France.

The uprooted Ndétare had followed the Serer maxim which states that the eyes and ears are the best guides. He'd watched and observed a long time, he'd listened hard, heard a great deal, and made the necessary effort to fit in. But he'd only partially assimilated. This island society, even when it allows an approach, remains an impenetrable monolithic structure that never digests foreign bodies. Here, everyone's alike. For centuries, the same genes have been running through the village, present in every marriage, defining the features of the island, producing successive generations which, one after the other, have shared the same lands in accordance with immutable laws. The distribution of surnames, with scarcely a variation, shows the precise map of neighbourhoods. This is what excluded Ndétare, the Senegalese man from the outside. He knew this micro-society would always spew him out the better to marginalise him. He'd noticed that some of the island's inhabitants barely had the IQ of a crustacean, but, being scorned, it was he, the intellectual, who'd at last found a link with this flotsam the Atlantic refuses to swallow, which washes up in the village.

Of course I remember Monsieur Ndétare.

On his roll-call, he'd encountered a surname as foreign as his, belonging to just one person in the village. He'd noticed his pupils' contempt as soon as he uttered this name. Since he was a good listener, he'd heard and decoded the murmuring at parent-teacher meetings: because she held her head too high, that woman, instead of looking around her and being satisfied with a son from a good family in the village, had gone elsewhere to choose a prince charming, who'd rewarded her with a bastard. Geographically insular, some of the islanders were mentally insular, too, and reproached my mother for having imported this foreign name to the village: not one of the founding ancestors had that name. The more moderate consoled themselves by declaring with a sarcastic laugh: 'Lucky for us she's a girl. There's no danger she'll spread her name among us.' Those who were aggravated by my good marks replied: 'Yes, but in the meantime she's stealing our children's opportunities. That foreigner probably has secret powers. After all, what do we know of her father?' At school, the kids took up their parents' ideas. The playground was often transformed into a battlefield and Monsieur Ndétare had finally located his black sheep. Pulling me out of yet another fight, he'd whispered: 'You'll always be a stranger in this village, like me, and you can't fight every time they make fun of your name. Anyway, it's a beautiful name, it means dignity; so show some dignity and stop fighting. You should stay in the classroom during break, and learn your lessons. With a bit of effort, one of these days you'll get out of this snake pit.'

For the first time I was proud of my name. That day, I asked my grandmother. She confirmed Ndétare's words and, in her own peculiar language, told me a story about my father's lineage that made me straighten my shoulders and carry my head high. I repeated that story word for word to my stepfather the day, under the palaver tree, with all the men from his neighbourhood present, he dared to call me by his name. I was ten years old at the time, and after that he never again looked me in the eye. My grandmother had taught me that if words are capable of declaring a war, they're also strong enough to win it.

Perhaps in solidarity, Ndétare paid special attention to my education. He'd waited in vain for an unlikely transfer to one of the big cities, where he wanted to continue his trade union activities. Then, seeing the years go by, he'd finally become resigned to ploughing our fallow brains. When his loneliness threatened his mental equilibrium, he'd go and sit on the jetty and scan the horizon of his Marxist ideas, which the sea washed back to rot at his feet. Occasionally, starved of affection, he thought he saw the silhouette of Sankèle, his long-lost love, among the dancing shadows of dusk. It was his only Niodior love story, one of those stories that leave you red-eyed. She'd left him with the taste of the island's sand in his throat and the heart of a lyric poet robbed of his muse. It had occurred a few years after he'd arrived; he'd remained a bachelor ever since, and his sheets were about as creased as an abbot's. To flee the private dialogue with his tormented soul, he'd turn up at all the customary ceremonies, seizing any opportunity likely to suck him into the whirlwind of village life. But he'd realised in the end that here, the palaver tree is a parliament, the family tree an identity card. The national constitution remains a virtual concept and people don't give a damn about it; it's the last remnant of the colonial dream that's sunk to the bottom of the Atlantic. Monsieur Ndétare was a foreigner, and would remain so for many years after his arrival in the village. His host family in Niodior was my grandmother and those close to her. So evening classes for Madické were the least he could do, considering the immense gratitude he felt towards the only family that had opened its arms to him, a family that had crept into his life through his classroom door, which he insisted on leaving open.

Like many island boys, Madické had attended only Koranic school and knew nothing of Ndétare's classes. His father considered it more worthwhile to learn to know God and to study the paths of salvation than to tie yourself up in knots decoding the whites' language. Madické had given up Koranic school as a teenager, along with most of his friends. Besides fishing and work in the fields, he devoted himself to football and to learning French. For his earthly salvation, he was willing to make an effort.

Training, Monsieur Ndétare! Monsieur Ndétare, French lessons! It sometimes happens that a person not tied to you by blood or love becomes the centre of your life, simply because he holds your hand and helps you to walk on the wire of hope along the trembling line of existence. A friend! Frantically. Calmly. Thank you! So Monsieur Ndétare had become the pivot for Madické's dreams and the subject of our telephone calls.

'Hello! Yes?'

'Yes, it's me, Madické. Call me back.'

'How are you? How are Grandma and Grandpa?'

'I'm OK. I've just finished training. Monsieur Ndétare says there's a chance we could win the Islands' Cup this year. We've already beaten Bassoul, two–one.'

'Not bad! Is everyone—'

'Everyone's fine. Monsieur Ndétare says that if we win the Islands' Cup, some of us could get into the regional team. A lot of Senegalese players abroad were picked from regional teams.'

'Oh yes? So did you get the parcel? There were your sports things and—'

'Yes, we got everything. Monsieur Ndétare says I have a chance, especially if I get better at French. Well, I've got to go. There's a match on the TV; AC Milan's playing at home; they'll be brilliant. Did you see Maldini's last match? He's on unbelievable form at the moment. Right, I'm off. Bye!'

Frustrated? Yes! I always was after Madické's phone calls. Never any news but his. Was he selfish? Say that and I'll cut out your tongue. My brother wasn't selfish, just passionate. Show me a passionate person who's aware that his hobby bores the other person to tears. When it comes to the lengths we go to for our passions, Madické, you and I are all the same. The sound of a beating heart drowns all the sirens of morality. A horse doesn't hear the noise his galloping makes. Only someone else's eye can detect the bit of dry snot hanging from our nose, the scrap of food at the corner of our lips, the bad breath, the messy hairdo, the ill-matched clothes, the habit of interrupting, spluttering, moaning over nothing and going crazy for everything – in short, only other people notice the thing we've got wrong, which stops us from being angels.

My brother was galloping towards his dreams, which centred more and more on France. He might have longed to go to Italy, but not a bit of it. The nation's sons who dine with the President play in France. Monsieur Ndétare, who was teaching him the language of success, had studied in France. The television he watched came from France, and its owner, the man from Barbès, a respectable, important man in the village, was full of marvellous tales of his odyssey.

5

IN THE MOONLIGHT, when the matches on the TV were over, the man from Barbès would lord it over his admiring audience and spin out his tales, while one of his wives passed at regular intervals with tea.

"So, uncle, what was it like over there, in Paris?" one of the young men would suddenly say.

This was the ritual question, the innocent formulation God required in order to recast the world under the starry Niodior sky.

'It was like nothing you could imagine. Like on TV, but better, because you see it all for real. If I told you what it was really like, you wouldn't believe me. It was magnificent, but the word doesn't do it justice. Even the Japanese come to take photographs of every corner of the capital. It's said to be the most beautiful capital city on earth. It was dark when I landed in Paris; you'd think the good Lord had given those people billions of red, blue and yellow stars to light them; the whole city was a blaze of lights. As the plane descended, you thought of all the people in their apartments. And I lived in that vast city, Paris. Their airport alone is bigger than our village. Before, I could never have imagined such a beautiful place existed. But now I was seeing it with my own eyes. It's as if the Eiffel Tower and the Obelisk touch the sky. You'd need a whole day at least to go down the Champs Elysées; it's lined with so many luxury shops crammed with extraordinary things to buy, you can't help window-gazing. Then there are very fine historical monuments – the Arc de Triomphe, for example – because you should know that whites are proud, and since they're so rich they put up a monument to mark even the least of their achievements. This helps them remember the great men in their history, too. What's more, they have a luxurious burial place for them, the Panthéon: it's fit for a prince – to think they put dead men in there! And then their God is so powerful He's given them untold riches; so to honour Him they've built churches everywhere, gigantic buildings with amazing architecture. The most famous, Notre Dame cathedral, is known throughout the world: thirteen million visitors a year! Beside that, our mosque looks like a hut. I'm told the great mosques of Dakar and Touba are very beautiful. I've never seen them. It's funny; I know Paris, but I don't even know Touba. Parisians who've come to Senegal for their holidays have told me the Touba mosque is one of the finest in Africa. I'll go and visit it one day, *insh'Allah*.'

'And what about life over there?'

The young listeners didn't care for his digressions. They wanted to hear about *over there*: where dead men sleep in palaces, surely the living must be dancing in paradise. So they pressed their narrator. Relishing the growing interest in his tale and spurred on by their curiosity, the man from Barbès sipped a cup of tea, displayed his toothless smile and went on, his voice still more animated.

'Ah! Life, over there! A real life of luxury! Believe me, over there they're very rich. Every couple lives with their children in luxury apartments, with electricity and running water. It's not like here, where four generations live under the same roof. Everyone has his own car to drive to work and take the children to school, his own television with channels from all over the world; his fridge and freezer stuffed with good food. Their life is very leisurely. Their wives don't do housework any more. They have machines to wash clothes and crockery. To clean the house they just go round it with a machine that swallows up all the dirt; it's called a vacuum cleaner, one suck and it's gone – bzzz! And it's spotless. So they spend their time making themselves beautiful. They put on skirts, short dresses, trousers and high heels at any hour of the day. They wear beautiful jewels, like the ones I brought back for my wives. And they're rich, too; they're not dependent on a man for food and shelter. No need to pay a dowry or ruin yourself for a wedding; they'll do anything you like, and, believe me, they have a talent for it. Their eyes are all different colours – it takes your breath away. Over there, on Saturdays, they take the car to go shopping, in wonderful covered markets, supermarkets, where you can find anything you can think of, even food that's already cooked, all you have to do is eat it. And the restaurants – well, now, they're something else! Their food's praised all over the world, it's so sophisticated. In some restaurants you can eat as much as you like. At home, you eat just as well, as much meat as you could wish for. They don't eat much grain, not rice with every meal like us. They eat a lot of pork, but that's not for us, so I'd have chicken, lamb or beef. And, of course, they have all kinds of drinks to go with their meals. And everyone lives well. Nobody's poor, because even those with no work are paid a salary by the state: they call it benefit. You spend the day snoozing in front of your TV, and you receive the same as one of our highest-paid engineers! So families can have a good standard of living; the state gives them money according to how many children they have. Therefore the more they procreate, the more money they make. Every night of love is an investment! I had a neighbour who didn't work, and neither did either of his wives, but with his ten children declared in his first wife's name he made more than me, and I had a job. Whites wouldn't need to work at all if they had lots of children, but they don't want as many as we do. Anyone can be rich over there; just look how much I have now. People make a lot of money there. Even the ones who pick up dog mess on the street are paid by the Paris city authorities. I could talk about it all night, but you can guess the rest. Your wildest dreams can come true. You'd have to be a real idiot to come back from there poor.'

The moon moved slowly across the Niodior sky, hypnotising the coconut palms, slowing the breath of people exhausted from a long day's struggle to survive. High heels echoed down the corridor of the huge house that belonged to the man from Barbès. The jangle of fake jewellery announced the arrival of his fourth wife, wearing western clothes, bringing the last round of tea and a tray of sliced mangoes. She eyed the group of boys who were only slightly younger than she was. If they didn't dare stare at her in front of her husband, her very presence aroused their desire. With her generous breasts and cute arse, she'd become the subject of their secret discussions. A momentary silence. The master of the house broke the ice: 'Hmm…Tell me, what did you put in the tea this evening? It's excellent!'

Madame wriggled and smiled by way of an answer. Perhaps she'd brewed up the tea with some grigri to arouse her man, on the advice of wise old women.

'Well,' said the man from Barbès, handing back the cup, 'you carry on. I'll be there in a minute. I think I'm going to need a massage this evening.'

It was always blackest night when Madické and his friends scattered down the alleyways of the sleeping village. Biting the inside of his cheek, the man from Barbès threw himself into bed, relieved that once again he'd succeeded in preserving, even consolidating, his status. He'd been a *nigger in Paris*, and as soon as he'd returned he'd set about sustaining the illusions that gave him an aura of success. Relying on the oral tradition to outdo all those who'd written about that city, he'd become France's best ambassador. He had no need of Madame's massage to get him going – his throng of heirs proved that, his millions aside, porn king Rocco Siffredi had nothing on him – but he had to have it, at least to delay the onset of the nightmare in which he saw himself with Pinocchio's nose. His entourage might swallow his lies, but his conscience dogged him, because it wasn't easy to present salt as sugar, even if they both have the same glint in the moonlight. However, since his ego eclipsed his remorse, he denied to himself he was lying: what harm was there in sifting through his memories, methodically selecting those that could be exposed and leaving the others to sink into oblivion? His flood of tales never hinted at the wretched existence he'd led in France.

How could he, sceptre in hand, have admitted that in the beginning he'd hung around the métro entrances, picked pockets to relieve his hunger, begged, only survived the winter thanks to the Salvation Army before finding a squat with his companions in misery? Could he describe the countless markets where, buttocks clenched every time the cops came by, he'd carry crates of fruit and vegetables, blindly obeying the slimy bastard who'd pay him under the counter with a crust of bread? As a perpetually illegal immigrant, he later travelled the length and breadth of France at the beck and call of less than scrupulous employers, equipped with a false residency permit, a photocopy of a friend and accomplice's residency card. He'd operated the pneumatic drill on building site after building site, in all weathers, always on fixed-term contracts. His muscles had strengthened, but it was his nerves that threatened to give. Since his French, which was not up to expressing subtleties, kept his brain cells out of play, he realised his body was his only capital and invested it in pumping iron. A giant now, he flexed his muscles and went for specific jobs. Though he was as meek as a lamb, his square jaw soon pegged him for a security guard. At night, he'd sharpen his eyesight on the surfaces of the gleaming cars in the underground car parks of swanky apartment blocks. I don't know who was walking who, but with a guard dog at the other end of the leash he'd pace the dark, grease-stained concrete until the first 'Morning, Sambo' signalled the end of his shift. Sambo was not his name, but that was what everyone in the apartment block called him.

According to the grapevine, the period synonymous with his emergence from the shadows – indeed, the acme of his career in France – was when he went from from being a dog's master to a guard dog: as night watchman in a big supermarket, he'd wander the aisles, salivating at the sight of goods that were beyond his reach. To avenge his frustration, he'd sniff out the thief among those of his fellow travellers he considered so arrogant as to do their shopping like whites, or too poor to be honest. Sometimes, North African or African prey would be gripped in his hawk-like talons, ensuring his boss's approval. His victims eventually came to understand that the foreigner's worst enemy isn't the native racist, that kinship doesn't guarantee solidarity. As his peace of mind grew, a gang from his estate decided to make him pay for his devotion to the rich: he left two teeth on the pavement. He's been waiting for the tooth fairy ever since, and when the two pearls missing from his smile are mentioned, he simply answers: 'Jutht a thmall acthident at work.' No one but the lone hunter knows what his quarry has cost him. If he returns smiling, the village merely praises his skill and bravery. The lion that gets away conceals his wounds beneath his lustrous hide. The man from Barbès did the same; there was no risk of a scratch to his veneer, he was sure of that: the adults envied him too much to nitpick, and the young boys' nails weren't strong enough to worry him. They were little pelicans thirsty for the blue yonder; they needed his beakfuls of colour to paint their skies. When they left him, at the end of those evenings, they showed gratitude and respect.

Not one of them would have missed the next day's training for anything in the world. There was no longer any doubt, they owed it to themselves to get to France. But for little illiterate village boys like them, there was precious little option; the only route open to them began on the football pitch - they had to kick their way there. Winning the Saloum Islands' Cup was only a formality now, so great was their determination. The little Niodior team crushed its adversaries one after the other. For some time Madické's phone calls contained no surprises. Though he told me about his progress in his evening classes and understood the French phrases I inadvertently dropped into our conversations more and more, he was always more voluble when it came to football. He'd announce cheerfully: 'We beat Thialane, one goal to nil.'

Or: 'We knocked out Djirnda two–nil. That was the score at the end of the first half.'

And finally: 'We smashed Dionewar in the final three–nil. We've won the Islands' Cup.'

The boys were riding high. Thrilled, Monsieur Ndétare would organise a party every so often to reward his troupe of champions. But instead of celebrating, the little band would pester him with questions. Would the scout for the region be coming to watch them play? Which of them had a chance of making the regional team? And, most important, who could hope to one day go and play for a French club? This last question annoyed the teacher. While he encouraged their zeal for football, he didn't much appreciate their desire to leave their country. He loved sport, and remained true to Coubertin's motto.

'*Citius, altius, fortius*!' he'd yell at them. 'Faster, higher, stronger! Play for the pure joy of it! Love the beautiful game, give it your all! The only aim is to better yourself, the only satisfaction applause. It's not about money, it's about self-realisation. That's the true spirit of sport, and that's how it is wherever you play. You don't need to go to France for that!'

Madické didn't believe this any more than his friends did, but he avoided contradicting the teacher, out of respect. But one young man, Garouwalé, nicknamed the Poker, was the cheekiest of the lot and pulled no punches: 'Yes, but you know, we still need to make money. What do you expect us to live on, then? At least, in France, you know exactly why you're playing; you're paid handsomely for your talent. Apparently, over there, the state pays people a salary even if they don't work. We want to go to France, and even if we don't have a great career in football, we can do what that guy who went to Paris did: we can always find work and bring back a small fortune.'

'Not so, my boy, not so. You're living in a dreamworld, not everyone brings back a fortune from France. Anyway, instead of listening to that braggart's nonsense, you should have asked Moussa to tell you his experience of France. He, too, listened to the siren song…'

And Ndétare began to relate Moussa's adventures in France.

6

ALL THAT REMAINED OF MOUSSA was a yellowed photo, sent from France, which Ndétare brandished before his protégés to authenticate his tale. In fact, of all the villagers the school-teacher was the only one who knew the full version of his story. When he'd come back, the young man had confided in him.

Every scrap of life must serve to win dignity!

The only son and eldest child of a big family, Moussa was sick of contemplating their poverty. Forced to leave school early to find work, the future had seemed to him a ravine leading to a black hole, for he had no idea what to put in the place of the air-conditioned civil servant's office he'd dreamed of for so long. But he wasn't a boy to give up easily. 'For the poor,' he'd say, 'living is like holding your breath under water, hoping you'll reach a sunny shore before the fatal gulp.' At twenty, having made up his mind to seek his fortune, he left the village for the town of M'Bour, on Senegal's Petite Côte, where he found work as a sailor on one of the big pirogues that fish on a small-scale. The young man was ambitious, he knocked at every door. He had too many mouths to feed, he couldn't make do with the unreliable income fishing provides. After several attempts, he managed to secure a place in the town's football team. He was a regular at training sessions and in matches he gave his all. He was quickly spotted by Jean-Charles Sauveur, a Frenchman who introduced himself as a talent scout for a big French club. Who said the good Lord was deaf?

The scout had no trouble convincing the young lad. He had only to lay his cards on the table: a plane ticket paid for by the club, guaranteed accommodation in the training centre where he'd be coached with the juniors before heading for fame playing for the great club – with, above all, the promise of a fabulous salary. The only obstacle was the boy's age: twenty was a little old to be taken on as a junior. The thorn was swiftly removed: here, you can arrange a second or even a third birth; a few banknotes behind the back of the chief clerk or handed to him in private will do the trick. In any case, nothing is refused someone who's going to France; he's a future contact worth having. Jean-Charles Sauveur, who was an old hand, produced the French francs at exactly the right moment. The visa? A mere formality! In embassies, too, there are greasy palms! Life in the tropics is so harsh! One of your countrymen passing through always smoothes the way. Bon voyage, gentlemen!

A few days later, Moussa was kicking a ball pumped with hope in a French stadium. It was only training, but to him it was the most important match of his life. For the first time ever, he was performing on a real football pitch, with dressing rooms and proper green turf. He was determined to astound the French coach, who scrutinised his every move: 'If we can bring on his game, with that build he'll demolish the opposition,' was his comment. And that's how it was in every training session that followed. Under Jean-Charles Sauveur's paternal eye, Moussa felt he was invested with a sacred mission. He must not falter; Sauveur was impatient for his talent to be confirmed so as to obtain the return on his outlay. At the centre in the evenings, watching TV,

Moussa was incensed at the buying and selling of players, and he'd end up ranting at the phenomenal transfer sums: Real Madrid bought that kid for how many million French francs? Wow! How much would that be in CFA francs? At least enough to buy five villas with swimming pools on the Dakar coast! Much as he enjoyed this calculation, imagining himself the object of such a transaction, he didn't like the process, which smacked of slavery. But he had no choice; he was part of this sporting cattle market now. Moussa knew that if he wasn't taken on by the club backing him, he'd have to reimburse Sauveur himself for the expenses he'd incurred: the plane ticket, bribes, accommodation costs, training etc. So he gave his all.

Every scrap of life must serve to win dignity!

All he knew of France was the training centre and the frozen turf. He could worry about sightseeing later; after all, he hadn't come to France for the châteaux. Soon, when his matches were broadcast on TV, when the Niodior kids could marvel at his prowess and he was at last invited to meet the Senegalese President, he'd be able to tour France in a Porsche, between championships. So there was nothing much to relate in the letter he wrote home. His parents, who, on their way to Ndétare's to have it read, were anticipating the adventures of Telemachus, only better, were sorely disappointed. The content of the letter was as thin as a report of the Paris–Dakar rally written by Johnny Hallyday. The schoolteacher translated:

Hello, everyone. I hope you're all well. I am fine. We train every day. I don't have a salary yet, but it shouldn't be long. God bless you and keep you! Pray for me.

Along with these seven brief sentences, the envelope contained a photograph taken at the only outing the centre had organised to show off the national team in action. His father, beside himself with anger, flung the photograph in the teacher's face, grumbling: 'You see! My son's barely arrived in France and he's already changed. Just look at that get-up! And he has the nerve to talk to me about a footballer's salary, as if he couldn't find himself a proper job. Grown men jumping around between four posts, he calls that work! May the Lord open his eyes! Ndétare, you're going to write me a letter for him right now. Put down exactly what I tell you.'

While his absence riled his father, Moussa was finding out about the harshness of winter, the wind biting his skin, the lack of sunlight, and the perpetual cold that often forced him to put his hand to his nose, even on the pitch. He was also finding out about his fellow players at the training centre, who were mostly whites and not exactly friendly. At the centre, no one gave a damn for team spirit. These boys were ambitious, and not everyone would make it. The trainees knew they wouldn't all be offered a contract. The few places at the club were fought over both on the pitch and off. You had to have nerves of steel. Moussa wasn't used to this kind of competition: back home, he'd been taught not to be envious, not to be jealous, not even to compete, that God alone grants to each his due in this life. Beyond the promise of success, Moussa expected only honest camaraderie and mutual respect from sport. He found only sordid calculation and contempt. On the pitch, he lost his cool when one of his team-mates shouted: 'Hey! Darkie! Pass! Come on! Pass the ball, it's not a coconut!'

In the dressing rooms there was always one who taunted him in front of the others: 'So? You think you've got balls? Don't worry, we'll show you. We'll take you to the Bois de Boulogne one of these nights. You'll be invisible, but you'll see everything.'

'Hey, guys, maybe he prefers Pigalle? Guess what, the

guy's never been to Paris and you know what he came out with last time? Oh yeah! Back when we were getting to know each other, Tarzan here, who's missing the jungle, wants to open up. So, guys, really want to know what he told me?'

'Give us a break!' yelled the ringleader. 'Spit it out. We need a laugh.'

'Well, he says some Jean-Baptiste, a famous eighteenth-century French sculptor, gave his name to Rue Pigalle! Hear that, boys?'

'Makes you wonder where he gets it. Don't tell me they talk about sculpture under the banana trees!'

'Hey, who knows? Maybe he was there at the time! Remember, that's where that prehistoric Lucy came from...'

'Instead of all that posing on the pitch, he should try running with the ball.'

Moussa resolutely turned his back on the tasteless jibes, restraining himself from punching whoever was responsible for the insults and jeering. *Take a deep breath, dive, swim to the sunny shore, keep going!* his inner voice hammered at him. As a good islander, he consoled himself with sayings from home: 'The waves may strike, they only sharpen the rock.' Months passed, and the rock of the Atlantic still hadn't surfaced. Recruited for his potential as a striker, Moussa had never scored even one goal, in spite of intensive training and his countless grigris. On match days he had to be content to polish the bench with his backside or make up numbers, often in positions that didn't allow him to show what he could really do. He admired the dressing rooms and enjoyed the hot showers, where he'd imagine beautiful moves he'd never been able to execute. He'd even invented his victory salute well before the glorious 1998 World Cup team. No, Moussa wouldn't have been satisfied with a vacant look and a finger pressed to his mouth, inviting the adoring fans to admire the striker's amazing prowess. That pantomime wasn't nearly expressive enough for his taste. A child of rhythm and the earth, he'd execute a frenzied *mbalax* before throwing himself on the turf, maybe even three somersaults to prolong the applause. But he never had the opportunity for that scene, rehearsed in his mind a thousand times, to come true. It wasn't just the cold which knotted his muscles but also the tremendous efforts he had to make to drag himself along with the homesickness that swelled in his stomach and left almost no room for the healthy food the centre provided. Long after the end of the adjustment period he'd been allowed, his performance was not up to scratch. The centre lost interest in him. Sauveur, sensing his investment was in jeopardy, made the first move.

'Listen, champ,' he told him, 'I've already spent enough on this, and you're really not getting anywhere. We're going to have to settle up. You owe me about a hundred thousand francs. You'll have to work for it. As you know, your residency permit's expired. If you'd done well, the club would have settled it all straight away: my money, your papers, all of it. But now you don't have a club or any other income, don't even think about your permit being renewed. I've got a mate with a boat; we'll go and see him. I'll get you a job down there. We won't ask for much; that way he won't blab. He'll hand your salary over to me, and when you've paid me back you can save enough to live it up back home. You're a strong lad, you'll be fine. But whatever happens, keep it quiet! Don't forget you have no papers. So one word and the cops'll have you in cuffs and you'll be playing your jazz in a dark cell. Mind you, you don't need a tan, do you? Now, tomorrow someone will come to take you to the boat. Once you're there, that's it, we've never met. Not a word to anyone! So long, champ.'

Moussa had only the evening to pack up his few possessions. Sauveur had seen fit to relieve him of the few masks that decorated his room. Gazing bitterly at the bare walls, poor Moussa seemed to wake abruptly from a long slumber: 'Shit, he's nicked all my sacred masks,' he said to himself. 'The guy's a real vulture. I'm not going on that damned boat. Those people will work me to death and never pay me a penny. I don't know where I'll go, but I'm getting the hell out before they come to get me.' Unable to sleep all night, he took out his father's last letter and read it again, out loud.

> *My son, I don't know if my letters have reached you, since I've still heard nothing from you. I saw your photo, you're not wearing a* thiaya *or a* sabador *now, and that worries me. Are your clothes hiding other changes in your personality? Nothing changes on the outside without changes on the inside. So I'm praying your soul has remained as pure as when you left. Never forget who you are and where you come from. When I say this, I mean you must continue to respect our traditions: you're not a white man. You're turning into an individualist like them. You've been in France for over a year now and you've never sent so much as a penny home to help us. To this day, not one of the plans we'd made when you left has been carried out. Life here is hard. Your sisters are still living at home. I'm growing old and you're my only son: it's your duty to look after your family. Spare us this shame among our people. You must work, save money and come home.*

When he finished reading the letter, Moussa lay down and determined to wait for the man who'd take him to the boat. He picked up the letter many more times and reread the end: *Spare us this shame among our people. You must work, save money and come home.*

He couldn't just take off. He closed his eyes to try to imagine the strength he'd need to be equal to what was expected of him. His next-door neighbour was listening to loud music, without melody or harmony; he knew nothing of the drama that lined the dividing wall. Lost in the cityscape, each tortoise drags his shell to the sound of his own breathing. The world of techno hears and waits for no man.

Moussa needed quiet. For the first time since he'd been at the centre, he thumped his fist on the wall. He flung himself onto the bed, hands folded across his chest. Closing his eyes, he felt his life rise up before him like the trunk of a baobab tree, impossible to embrace. Quiet. He needed quiet to be able to invent another destiny for himself, a new music for his dreams, to make his heart beat to a rhythm other than the blues. Quiet at last! But he didn't need quiet to hear his family's deafening complaint. The echoes of a phrase that the drone of the waves has washed over his village since time immemorial resounded over and over, deep in his skull: *Every scrap of life must serve to win dignity!* And that phrase dictated the next: *You must work, save money and come home.*

Work? Once on the boat, that was all Moussa did. Work, work and more work, until homesickness sweated from his pores. The only smells in this country were the stench that emanated from the depths of the hold and the sour smell from the robust bodies of his workmates, who were as roughly shaven as he was. For Moussa, the sophistication of French cuisine had no meaning. His stomach stored only the tasteless meals served up by a cook who blew his nose with his fingers while he peeled the potatoes, a sailor who had no qualms about running to the latrine between main course and dessert. And yet, being stoical, he told himself that after all it wasn't so bad: he was fed and had a roof over his head. This way, after he'd paid back Sauveur, he'd be able to save all his wages and return home when he considered himself rich enough. For a long time the beauty of France appeared to him in the guise of a few multicoloured lights glimpsed from the port. When, months later, his curiosity led him to take advantage of a stopover in Marseilles to see up close what there was in France besides stadium turf and the depths of the hold, the bells of the old town tolled his nuptials with Fata Morgana, death knell to all his dreams. He didn't know it yet, but every step brought him closer to the funeral pyre of his hopes. A true *guelwaar*, he strolled along with pride, hands in pockets, his eyes greedy for images, his lungs breathing easily, carried along by the town planners' imagination. Only at the last moment did he notice the welcome committee who'd spotted him by his air of wonderment and had been following him for the last dozen metres.

'Show us your ID!'

Surprised by this order, he turned round and saw a kepi above bushy eyebrows and two pools of blue. A timid sun risked a last wink and tiptoed away to report back to God.

'I said your ID, sunshine!'

'The boss has it,' he said confidently.

'What boss might that be, and where is he?' shouted the other kepi.

'The boss of the boat, over there, in the port,' he assured them.

'Well, what do you know?' remarked the first kepi. 'Our friend's royalty; he needs someone to carry his papers for him. Come on, let's go and check it out. I suppose his mum still wipes his arse too.'

At the port, the boss had no idea who his sailor was. In fact, he'd never seen him before. A model French citizen and honest boss, his credentials were impeccable: he avoided illegal workers like the plague, it went without saying.

Moussa, escorted by his guides in blue, began his tour of French bureaucracy. He left the port as the stars pricked the velvet shadow of night, which struggled to lend human beings its tenderness. This was the hour at which the cabin boy would be serving supper to his galley mates, who wouldn't be venturing on to dry land during stopovers again. He climbed obediently into the police car with not the least idea of the damp, foul-smelling cell that awaited him. He spent some days there, telling himself that anywhere on the planet would be more bearable than this tiny hole where his illusions, weary of spinning around, returned to wrap themselves around already numb limbs. A fisherman by chance, he was trapped in fortune's nets. His horizon liquefied beneath his long black eyelashes. This was his Bermuda Triangle. A Sahelian, who loved the sun and the ocean breeze, he'd have given anything to be able to run about, even in Siberia. Confronted with the revolting food that the warden brought - that slop of the conscience of the country that invented human rights - he even found himself missing the purée with snot served up on the boat. The hardest part for him was the lack of activity. So, to pass the time, he'd stretch out on his back and delve into his imagination, changing himself into a spider spinning its web, not to catch his fugitive dreams but to fill in the many cracks in the four walls and ceiling. He enjoyed this exercise, which helped make his notion of space relative: his metamorphosis into a little beast made the available space gigantic and modified his perception of time. When a passing warden dragged him from his reverie, the all-too-obvious reality filled him with bitterness. He was overcome with longing, and his aborted plans performed for him like demonic dancers. To stare them down, he lined them up along the walls, each with a crack of its own; so he could inspect them clearly, one at a time, he gave each fissure the name of a plan. Thus, with the intricacy of gossamer, words wove the line necessary for one idea to follow on from another. Being a Muslim, he named the cracks from right to left, in decreasing order of priority: build a big family home, invest in a motorised pirogue for the village, open a grocery shop for his mum – that way there'll always be something to eat – save up for a bride, buy clothes for the whole family, especially jewels and luxury perfumes for his betrothed, pay for plane tickets for his parents to make the pilgrimage to Mecca etc.

Little by little, his desires covered the cell and finally hid the cracks from him. When he grew tired of contemplating them, the lessons from his teacher at Koranic school revealed their only use: to bring him closer to his Creator through prayer. *Allah Akbar!* The path that led to this God, to whom he gave thanks five times a day, was surely shorter than the width of the residency card that lay between him and freedom and even perhaps the fulfilment of his dream. *Alhamdoulilah!* Moussa was awaiting God's help. *Insh'Allah!* But it was a French government euphemism that eventually greeted him in the depths of his cell. One morning a policeman arrived, smiling broadly, and threw an official paper at him with a flourish: 'There you go, your invitation!'

It was an IQF, an Invitation to Quit France. Twelve hours later an aeroplane spat him out on the tarmac at Dakar airport. This was his homecoming, his dreams of prosperity left behind in his cell, enriched only with the power of meditation, a helpless love of spiders and an image of France never seen on postcards.

Seeking consolation, he made his way back to the village thanks to the generosity of a close relative who'd been so kind as to give him enough to pay his bus ticket. His parents were overjoyed to see him. Then, giving him no time to answer, they asked why he hadn't let them know; they could have given him a proper welcome! No one suspected his plight, despite the absence of luggage. He must have been impatient to see the family and had sent his many bags separately; he'd be going to Dakar later to collect them. Optimism sacrificed a rooster to give thanks to the ancestors, as well as two ducks for the evening meal. The excitement muzzled Moussa throughout the three long days of festivities. Unable to let his family run any further into debt to honour him, he gave a brief summary of his experience of France. The explosion of truth covered him in ashes. He no longer shone with European light and was now of less interest than even the most sedentary islander. Almost everyone despised him. Even the village idiot berated him: 'Everyone who's worked over there built houses and shops as soon as they came home. If you haven't brought anything back, it's because you're a failure.'

Moussa knew this simpleton was only cheekily echoing the general chorus. Everybody knows the idiot is the frankest person in the village; it's well known. Moussa rarely went out, avoided public places and took refuge in a silence from which he only emerged when Ndétare invited him for tea. Having found in the schoolteacher the only island dweller who still paid him any attention, Moussa confided in him and wallowed in his sympathy. He'd sometimes accompany him to the football pitch and watch the training, in silence. The boys, who'd idolised him in the days when he'd been the local Platini, concentrated on their game, pretending not to see him. The magnanimous Ndétare always set an extra place at his table. To escape his parents' guilt-inducing looks and his sisters' obvious disdain, Moussa spent most of his time with the schoolteacher.

The tide was rising. The Atlantic's waves struck and polished the mangrove but, no matter how hard they tried, they never gave the mud the radiance of white sand. The tide was rising. With it, the noise of the waves that swept the mire along. The tide rose. The breeze spread putrid, as always, over the whole village.

Not knowing why the government had exiled the schoolteacher on the island, banning him from the city, people looked to his way of life for the reason. His friendship with Moussa gave rise to speculation. This urban man, still a bachelor at an age when the rest of his generation were watching their progeny grow, had lived with the whites for a long time while he was studying. Moussa, too, was transformed since he'd come back from over there. There had to be a reason other than mere friendship for the two men spending so much time together. They'd been seen walking together at dusk by more than one villager. They must be indulging in unwholesome activities, in secret, activities they'd picked up from the whites. And it was this, it was said, that kept them aloof from the rest of the community. The tide rose even higher. Soon, the water-sodden fencing could hardly stand in the mud. Slowly but inexorably it began to sag. Moussa could hear it murmuring: 'Atlantic, carry me away. Your harsh belly will be softer to me than my bed. Legend says you give shelter to those who seek it.'

Moussa, like all those native to the island, had heard this legend as a boy.

There was once a man living in the village who went by the name of Sédar. One day, his mother-in-law, who blamed him for not giving her grandchildren, revealed his impotence in the village square. Mortified, the son-in-law left the village. Arriving at the beach, his arms open to the ocean, Sédar shouted: 'Atlantic, carry me away. Your harsh belly will be softer to me than my bed!'

The waves closed over him. But when he did not come back, his wife, Soutoura, who loved him passionately, went out to look for him. It had rained the night before and she had only to follow his tracks in the sand. When she reached the beach, she saw her husband's clothes at the water's edge and began to scream: 'Sédar! Sédar, my love, come back to me!'

A dolphin emerged from the waves and said to her: 'My

dearest Soutoura, the world of men is narrow; only the ocean can cover my shame. Find another husband, one who's gentle and kind. I've left the realm of men; be sure never to tell them what became of me. I will remain their friend and I'll come to visit your children.'

But to twist a leash for words you must know how to weave the wind. To be certain she'd never betray her beloved husband's secret, Soutoura immediately flung herself into the surf. Like Sédar, she in turn was changed into a dolphin. Ever since, dolphins can be seen along Niodior's coast, in pairs or accompanied by their young. They have remained man's friends.

No longer daring to go to the schoolteacher's, Moussa shut himself away, telling himself the legend over and over. Weeks passed, each identical to the one before. After the Saturday match, to revive their aching limbs, the young footballers would go to the beach and dive into the sea. As the sun went down, they'd sing and splash around noisily. The schoolteacher's lanky form could be seen gesticulating frantically to get them out of the water. This happened every week, but on that particular Saturday, Ndétare had no need to lose his temper to make them leave the water.

The sun seemed to want to smooth out the sea's red wrinkles, the muezzin chanted the evening call to prayer. Thump! Thump! Thump! The last poundings of pestles vainly attempted to rouse the dead, who lay buried at the far ends of the village. Suddenly, making its last turn, a pirogue leaned to starboard to set its prow for the wharf. Seeing it, the group of boys split into two ranks, which then closed again in its wake.

The sand on the beach exuded mercy. Flat, white, fine and porous, it let the waves come timidly to suck its soul. Wood and other flotsam drifted out to the open sea on the crest of waves dancing backwards, hoping for an unlikely return to dry land. The branches of the mangroves fringing the beach pointed downwards, like flags at half-mast. These trees, which tirelessly contemplate their shadows when not merged with them, were stuck there in the hope of one day seeing their leaves, their branches, all those bits of themselves the sea made off with, return to them. Perhaps this wait is not in vain, since the sea gives back to the earth what belongs to it.

The pirogue moored. The breeze blew over the wounds of the living. Two fishermen silently unloaded their cargo. The young footballers approached. A man with strong arms lay stretched out on the wharf; from a distance, he looked like someone relaxing in the sun. Only his half-open clothes showed he hadn't chosen to be there, still less in that posture. Not far from the village, just at the place where the island dips its tongue into the sea, the fishermen had caught Moussa's inert body in their nets.

Even the Atlantic can't digest all that the earth throws up. *Allah Akbar!* In the mosque, prayers were over. The preacher ended his sermon with these words: *Every scrap of life must serve to win dignity!*

Nor could Ndétare's memory absorb Moussa's adventure. It stuck in his throat every time his protégés, pleading their passion for football, let themselves be blinded by the red, white and blue chimera. As a good teacher, he'd drowned his bitterness deep in his Cartesian soul and made use of the story as a cautionary tale.

'Be careful, my boys,' he'd conclude. 'Go and watch that upstart's TV, but please don't listen to the nonsense he spouts. France is not paradise. Don't get caught in the net of emigration. Remember, Moussa was your brother, and you know as well as I do what happened to him.'

Madické and his friends listened to the schoolteacher endlessly drumming the same words into them, without really hearing them. Isn't that what teachers do, talk a lot? To their minds, Ndétare was getting old; all he did now was witter on. So, when he started getting heavy, as they called it, the little team kept their distance, preferring to lose themselves in their dreams. Some made the most of this halt in their training to go to watch matches in the city; others went to consult marabouts who specialised in football. With their paltry savings, they bought themselves charms that were supposed to win them matches and help them make it to France one day. Every plant was invested with a power, and picking it accompanied by incomprehensible chanting. More and more herbal infusions were brewed up. Chickens' throats were slit according to complicated rituals. Under the moon's chaste gaze, a shadowy sorcerer administered purifications that were far from orthodox. Those who couldn't afford to recompense the 'wise men' turned to their mothers, who, prepared to do anything to improve their sons' futures, let themselves be fleeced: 'Farewell, finery and party dresses! There'll be others, when my son comes back from Europe a rich man!' Sssh! Don't whisper a word. Here, no one consults a marabout. A shadow has no name! At night, only spirits are abroad in the village.

During these breaks, Madické would call me more often, asking for football magazines. It didn't much matter what language they were in, so long as there was a picture of Maldini looking his best. But he was no longer content just to cover the walls of his room with posters of his idol. Whereas for his friends football was a means of reaching the west to get any job they could, Madické wanted to go to France to light up the stadiums with his talent. After all, hadn't he become the best player in the village team? With a bit of luck, a big French club would sign him up. And then, since Italy was right next to France, he could go and watch AC Milan matches, and maybe one day shake his hero's hand. *Insh'Allah!* Then he would come back home, proud, rich and happy. For him, France was simply the quickest route to Maldini's throne.

As in the France–Italy matches when he'd keep his forecasts to himself, he kept quiet when, to justify their desire to emigrate and shut up their teacher, his friends outlined their fabulous plans. How could he have explained to them that he, too, wanted to leave for Europe, to work and make a living, of course, but mostly to shake someone's hand?

Ndétare interpreted this silence as the meagre result of his perseverance. As a good teacher, he told himself that his diatribes were still of use as long as he could hope to save one of them. And then, he thought, if Madické could be brought to his senses, it would help him convince the others to give up their obsession. To convince himself, he adopted an island proverb that had originally done the rounds to put the young footballers' parents on their guard against the western influence that he himself might exert over their children: *A good convert makes the best preacher.*

But for the moment Ndétare had to spread the word alone and without great success. The boys still went to watch television at the house of the man from Barbès and would come home later and later. Their desire for the good life grew from one evening to the next, although the schoolteacher used every opportunity to wear them down with his refrain: 'Boys, don't listen to the nonsense that crackpot comes out with. Don't get caught in the emigration trap. Remember, Moussa was your brother...'

7

THE VILLAGE TEAM WAS BEGINNING to break up. The boys still loved football but were finding their coach's remarks increasingly galling. Who was he to ruin their dreams? Couldn't he understand they wanted to save their future, which the island's sand threatened to swallow up? What could he know of their poverty, their fish couscous every evening, their anxious parents who depended on them to keep them in their old age? In his teacher's quarters, what could he hear of their mother's nocturnal sobbing when there was nothing to put in the pot? He at least had his state salary each month. So he should keep his stoicism and fine ideas to himself. How easy it is to philosophise on a full stomach! They'd had enough of sucking their cheeks and making up magic spells to transform dried fish into red steak. They were more than determined. *Every scrap of life must serve to win dignity!*

Anyway, Ndétare's arguments were easy to demolish: it was jealousy that made him accuse the man from Barbès of lying, or perhaps he bore him a grudge; anyhow, they never spoke to each other. And the boys were beginning to get sick of hearing that Moussa story. Of course the poor guy had been unlucky, but that was no reason to discourage the rest of them. They'd seen other migrants who'd made it, besides the man from Barbès. Indeed, the richest native of the island was a former migrant who now lived in the city, where he owned several villas. It was at Moussa's funeral, in fact, that they'd met this man. All the villagers envied him, and for once the man from Barbès had kept a low profile.

This success story went by the name of El Hadji. He'd been called this since his return from the pilgrimage to Mecca, but his real name was Wagane Yaltigué. With the honorary title of El Hadji, his three wives and many fishing boats, all with powerful motors, Wagane aspired to be a dignitary. His pirogues stirred the admiration of the young footballers, all of them fishermen's sons. In their eyes, this man was the epitome of success. Wagane knew this and delighted in it. His every movement, the rustle of his long, well-starched *boubou*, reminded the villagers of all that life held beyond their grasp: wealth. He also knew that if he included the jealous and hateful, his enemies were as plentiful as the hairs in his beard. So, to provoke their envy, from time to time he'd roll up the sleeves of his robe, revealing a gold watch that shone mocking reflections into covetous eyes. When it was time for lunch, seated opposite his neighbours around the bowl, Wagane would wolf down his food with confidence. Unlike some of them, who'd modestly lower their heads, whether from respect for people's grief or to hide yellow teeth or a thinning beard, he'd brazenly bare his gold teeth.

Before he flew to France, during his brief stay in M'Bour, Moussa had worked on one of Wagane's pirogues. But this wasn't the only reason for the appearance of the former villager, now a rich city man. Many times before, his fishing crews had lost one of their number, and he hadn't felt obliged to attend the funeral. One might say the death of some of his employees had affected him less than the loss of a net. After all, there'd be poor men ready to trawl the belly of the Atlantic to earn their crust until the end of time; they turned up in droves at the fishing port every day. Moussa and his workmates would take all they could from the sea, and, when it avenged itself by swallowing one or several of them, the rest of the crew could do nothing but accept it. El Hadji Wagane Yaltigué would promptly reconstitute his workforce by recruiting among the dozens of candidates who waited on the docks, ready to risk their lives for a few sea bream. The frequent loss of entire crews wasn't sufficient to give work to all these men, who were jealous when they saw the sun patiently make love to the sea, a sea they'd wooed for days on end, with only their black skin to offer it. Quite often, this creature of their dreams would deign to give herself to them, draped in a sky-blue wedding dress whose train concealed a vast tomb. No doubt this was why Moussa had wanted to move on to something else.

Wagane Yaltigué didn't throw his fistful of earth on just any corpse; he'd come to Niodior because the dead man's father, despite his poverty, was a traditional dignitary, and it was advantageous to be counted among those close to him. This funeral gave Wagane the chance to strut before a select public and rub shoulders with the big boys. He was a clever strategist, behaving like those showbiz personalities who attend burials more for the cameras than to express any affection for the deceased. So, at the meal, El Hadji had naturally sat with the people who appeared to have high status. He was accepted without too much reticence. In the end, recognition has always been a matter of negotiation. Since his return from France, Wagane seldom came to the village, but each of his arrivals was a flash of lightning that blinded all the inhabitants. If the older men had given up trying to raise themselves to his level, the younger ones, on the other hand, would imagine themselves in his place. Originally from a very poor and humble family, he'd become one of the most powerful men in the region and, though some islanders made a show of austere pride, they were happy to profit in town from the benefits to be gained simply by claiming to be related to him. Besides, it was the only way for them to take advantage of the success of this relative who was ashamed of his roots, who'd abandoned them, they said, to make his home in the city.

Yet more than one had already benefited from his assistance by going to see him on the quiet. But the thing they couldn't forgive was his refusal to grant their more costly requests. His relatives and friends had tried in vain to borrow the price of a ticket to send their sons to France. Knowing that debts within the clan often remain unpaid, Wagane, ever the good businessman, had turned a deaf ear. They bowed low before him, but the moment his back was turned the waves were unleashed, carrying the same words: miser, selfish monster! And the swell amplified the echo of what mouths didn't dare utter: let him die, he can't take it with him! Nocturnal shadows hovered in the village. The marabout kept a late vigil, slipped a grigri into a skull in return for a few woollen stockings that left the conspirators penniless. But Wagane still inhaled the smell of his banknotes, despite the accusing looks. However greedy the lion, he's always good enough to leave the carrion to the vultures: so as to polish his image, Wagane left a sum of money to the imam, a contribution to the mosque's renovation and, for the village team, he'd brought a real football and more shirts than were needed. The boys thought him modern and generous, and now, during training, he was all they talked about.

Wagane also knew that every good dignitary has to have his personal griot. In the village, the old fisherman, who owed him his livelihood, sang his praises in spite of everything. Wagane had provided for him by letting him have an old motorised pirogue that could no longer venture out of the sound. His belly full of muddy carp, the old boy followed the training sessions from a distance. When the fish remains irritated his gums, he'd call out to the boys, to give his mouth some air and annoy the schoolteacher: 'You're adults now! You won't get to be respectable heads of families by kicking up the dust for nothing. You're wasting your time with this guy. Look at Wagane; now, he's a real role model, a worthy son of our village. He's been to the ends of the earth to make his fortune; now he's spreading it around. Leave, go where you can, but seek success instead of staying here, just to keep this depraved westernised man company. If he had a son your age, do you think he'd have him running around for no reason, like you are now? I don't think so! He'd have turned him into a civil servant already, like him, a performing parrot, paid to instil the whites' language and customs in you and make you forget our own! Go and look for work, get away from this dirty coloniser and don't forget, my sons, *every scrap of life must serve to win dignity*!'

To the schoolteacher's great annoyance, Moussa's death, instead of deterring the boys, had brought them closer to a man whose success more than vindicated their desire to emigrate. The old fisherman, like others it was true, was merely fanning the flames. But he filled Ndétare with a rage so intense it stunned the little team. The budding champions thought their coach's reaction excessive. They were too young to have heard about what divided the two men, beyond their differing opinions on emigration. Baffled, they went their separate ways, leaving the two adults to spit in each other's face words that should never have been included in the dictionary. Accustomed to seeing the teacher calm and conciliatory with the villagers, the boys wondered why he was so aggressive when it came to the man from Barbès and the old fisherman. Afraid to ask him, they made do with hearsay and went off to amuse themselves elsewhere. The old man was given to quarrelling, but he was no fool, so he followed close behind, escaping the fury of an adversary who was younger and stronger than he was. It's no cowardice to save your own skin, they say in the village; in fact, it's proof of intelligence.

As soon as his antagonist had disappeared from view, Ndétare went to the jetty to calm down. Sitting there, he watched the dead leaves float back to be caught in the mangroves. Silent and cold, the last waves of the day lapped at his legs, which he dangled idly in the water. Ndétare was doubly a prisoner: of this island, which he was forbidden to leave, but also of his memory, which had never let him feel anything but melancholy for so long now. Alone, facing the water, he drifted like a boat out into the murky sea of his memories.

That year, God had blessed the earth, multiplied the rains and freed people of all fear of famine: the crops had kept the men on dry land for longer than usual. When they finally had time to take the boats out, the waves simply pushed the shoals of fish into their nets. The Serer proverb, according to which God puts food in every mouth He creates, turned out to be true. Optimism was in the air; people thought only of procreating. The long hours of labouring in the fields, with the cooperation it encourages, brought families closer together, inspiring them to strengthen ties. The year was an especially auspicious one, ideal for weddings.

In the evenings the young women would come out at the same time as the stars to make their way to Dingaré, the village square. There, under the benevolent gaze of the moon, mother to them all, they'd make up songs, trying to outdo each other in grace and imagination. For nothing in the world would they have missed these night dances. Behind closed doors at school, they composed saucy tunes vaunting their charms, and love poems intended for their prince charming. Their nightingale voices caressed the tops of the coconut palms, and their delicate heels drummed the warm sand; the roll of the tom-tom beat out their destinies. At the same time, unbeknown to them, inside the houses the patriarchs were holding meetings that were utterly devoid of poetry. In line with ancestral law, they were selecting husbands for them, according to family interests and immutable alliances. Here, it's rare for two lovers to marry, but two families are always brought together: the individual is merely a link in the clan's all-powerful chain. Any breach in community life is quickly filled with a marriage. The bed is simply the natural extension of the palaver tree, the place where previously concluded agreements come into force. The highest pyramid dedicated to traditional diplomacy comes back to that triangle between a woman's legs.

Except that Sankèle, the old fisherman's daughter, intended to make her triangle the sanctuary of a free love: a consensual love that ignored community interests. Within her family, her keen mind and legendary beauty fuelled the hope of forging links with one of the most envied families in the village, whose son lived in France. Sankèle was barely seventeen when, without consulting her, her father and uncles chose her a husband, the man from Barbès, who'd returned from France for his first holiday at home. It was a good match; he lived in Europe and his family no longer depended on the harvest being plentiful. More than one father wished to give him his daughter's hand. And many were the songs made up in his honour by young women willing to follow him to the end of the world. But the beautiful Sankèle was addressing her mysterious poetry to quite another prince. Monsieur Ndétare, the schoolteacher, was her beloved. And it was with horror that she learned, from her father's lips, the news of her *takke*, her religious betrothal, to be celebrated at the mosque towards the end of the man from Barbès' holiday. Sankèle screamed loudly enough to tear her lungs: 'No, Father! No, I don't want anything to do with that monster. He's too old, too ugly. And what's more he's going away, far away. I'll never marry him, I'd rather die.'

'Your mother said the same thing,' he retorted, 'yet she gave me the most beautiful daughter in the village. Your fiancé is going away, but one day he'll take you with him to France, which will benefit all of us.'

In her fury, Sankèle performed the famous storm dance, still imitated by the Niodior palms: as she wept, she thrust her body violently from left to right, forward and back. But neither her tears nor her refusal to eat for several days made her father's determination waver. He planned for the marriage ceremony to take place as soon as her fiancé next returned, in two years' time. In the morning, he'd come to wish his daughter good morning. Huddled in a corner of her room, she'd invariably repeat: 'I don't love him, Father. I don't want that beast. Please, Father…'

'When the princess is alone with the beast, the story goes, she ends up loving him,' he'd declare without looking up.

Only her mother, caught up in memories of her sad youth, seemed to understand: she consoled her, while urging her to obey her father. She herself had lost her appetite, but at meal-times she'd bring her daughter a steaming bowl of food. The girl barely touched it, but that didn't stop her mother trying again and again. As everyone knows, a mother's stomach is in the belly of her child.

Tired of begging her father, Sankèle decided to fight. First, she had to renew contact with her beloved Ndétare. She needed his support, but he never came to see her, no doubt because walls had ears. By sending Ndétare, that troublesome trade unionist, into the belly of the Atlantic, the government hoped to see him sink, along with his ideals. But ideas are lotus seeds; they sleep only to grow stronger. Ndétare held firm and valiantly ploughed his furrow: keep on teaching, always, plant ideas in every fallow brain. He enjoyed spending hours telling his beloved about the great historical figures of all the different resistance movements, including feminism. So Sankèle, despite being illiterate, had naturally acquired a sense of revolt. To everyone's surprise, she stood up to her family, determined to refuse this imposed marriage to the end. Defying taboos, she found tenderness and comfort at Ndétare's side. With him, she secretly tasted the intoxication of requited love, a delight unknown to most of her friends, who began to be shocked by her frequent absence from the night dances. Her mother grew anxious as she came home later and later, long after the last beat of the tom-tom. She'd wait for her in the doorway, then, the moment she saw her emerge from the shadows, would plaintively call out: 'Be careful, Sankèle! Don't shame us in the village! Everyone's talking about you. If you do something stupid before you're married, we'll be lost. Your father will never forgive me, and he'll kill you – it's sharia law.'

Sankèle had not waited to do something stupid. She'd decided to make Ndétare the first. This honour she could offer only to the one she loved. But refusing her virginity to the stallion who'd been chosen for her wasn't the sole aim of her manoeuvre. Since diplomacy is fine-tuned between a woman's thighs, declarations of war may also issue from there. Sankèle knew this. To become an unmarried mother was the most radical way to reduce her father's matrimonial strategy to dust.

Ndétare welcomed this initiative. For him, the foreigner condemned to remain on the island, it was the only conceivable means of snatching a village girl's hand from her family.

They continued their tender nocturnal trysts. The rain was unceasing and the seed grew without warning.

Sankèle, fulfilled yet anxious, had managed to hide her condition until the beginning of the fifth month. With no gynaecologist, nor the scan's spying eye, the larva embedded itself and waited for the body to speak. Sankèle had been able to silence hers by tying her *pagne* a little tighter. She was betrayed by her breasts, which became udders to quench the thirst for life of a baby who'd neglected to ask permission to be born. If her mother cooked more slowly because her ladle kept filling with tears, her father's eyes were dried by the Etna in his heart. After thrashing Sankèle in front of her helpless mother, he decreed, as absolute master: 'You will not leave this room until, until…Well, you're staying here! Understood?'

Sankèle had understood, and so had her mother: the news of the pregnancy must not spread. What they hadn't worked out, however, was how to keep the baby's birth a secret. The mother tried to reason with her husband: 'But…'

He leaped at her and silenced her with a resounding slap, shouting: 'Shut up! You've always spared her the punishments she deserved! And now look what your lack of discipline has cost us! That slut's her mother's daughter for sure! One more word and I'll throw you out!'

In this corner of the earth, a man's hand is placed over every woman's mouth. So be it!

But Sankèle's mother didn't have to force herself to be silent for long. A few months after her husband's threat, she lost the power of speech for good.

There was a full moon that night, and neither Sankèle nor her mother were sleeping: someone was knocking at the door to the world.

The dogs were barking in an unusual way. The owl sang of things that men did not know – it's said here that eaters of souls change into owls at night and relate their deeds in long screeches. The neighbour's goat licked its kid. In the distance, the wolves lay in wait for the lamb that had unwisely strayed from the flock. The sea, woken by hunger, bellowed, chewed at the earth and demanded its toll of humans from the Niominkas, as Minos had from the Athenians.

Someone was growing impatient and knocking at the door to the world.

Sankèle, bathed in sweat, gave a dignified moan. She was forbidden to yell out in pain, since she was responsible for the greatest pain of all: family dishonour.

Someone was forcing the door to the world.

Sankèle clung to her mother, clenched her teeth and began to groan: 'Aaah! Ma-ma!'

'Quiet!' commanded her father, stationed behind his wife, a plastic bag in his hand.

The mother started. What was he doing there, holding that bag? Was he going to the grocer's to fill it, in exchange for a few CFA francs, with the powdered sugar that is added to the millet and palm oil porridge given to women who have just given birth? Tradition demanded that he should not be present at this rite, which has always been one of the rare privileges left to women.

'You vomit where you eat!' he added sententiously.

'Come on, my love, be brave, one more little push, it's nearly over,' the mother murmured, holding back her tears.

Someone pushed the door to the world.

A trembling hand cut the umbilical cord and offered the reckless guest a throne of white cotton. In spite of the care they took with him, he seemed to have understood that he was being asked not to disturb the silence of the world. His first cry was timid and soon hushed; a few drops of sugared water, in which a root had been steeped, were placed on his tongue. He sucked his tiny hands that, not knowing which end of life to grab hold of, returned to protect his little face. If it wasn't for his size, he could have been taken for a boxer: his sullen, bluish face seemed to have just dodged Mike Tyson's fists. To think we're so soppy over newborns that we exclaim: *Oh, he's so cute!* They're never beautiful; it's birth in itself that's beautiful.

Sankèle got her breath back. She looked down at her son, trying to make out the face of her beloved. Her mother picked up a basin and went to pour some water from the huge earthenware pot in the corner of the yard. As she returned to the room, a piercing scream split the warm earth beneath her feet. Rooted to the spot, she saw Sankèle rush past her holding her head in her hands. She tried to catch up with her but could not. She turned back to go and take care of the infant. The sight that greeted her robbed her of speech for ever after: her husband had put the baby in the plastic bag and was trussing him up like a joint of pork. Before his wife's bewildered gaze, he coldly announced: 'No illegitimate child will be raised under my roof.'

He left the room, his bundle under his arm, and made his way to the shore. After placing the little body in his pirogue, he rowed out to the open sea. When he considered he was far enough from shore, he secured the body with a big stone, hurled it to the bottom of the Atlantic and rowed back in his own wake.

Some dolphins, accompanied by their young, dived behind the pirogue. They've remained man's friends. Sometimes, they come near the village and seem to enjoy racing the boats. Legend has it that Sédar and Soutoura have a big family now: they turn drowned babies into dolphins and adopt them.

The old fisherman had barely crossed the threshold of his house when the reedy voice of the muezzin set the cocks crowing. The breath of dawn dispersed the blue of the night. He washed, picked up his beads and made his way to the mosque. *Allah Akbar!*

From that day on, his wife took refuge in the fortress of silence, letting her tears speak for her. Sankèle was never again seen sinking her little feet in Niodior's white sand. Her frantic dash had come to an end at Ndétare's door. He, unable to see any way to help his lover, resigned himself to facilitating her escape: he must save Sankèle, assist in her leaving the village. If the island is a prison, its whole circumference can provide an emergency exit. A land-dweller, the schoolteacher had no boat and was no sailor. The men were still at the mosque when he knocked at the door of his boatman friend, one of Madické's uncles. The boatman needed no persuading. He told Ndétare to take Sankèle over to the other side of the village, to the wild shore fringed with mangrove, where people seldom went. Then he went to the landing stage, untied a boat and circled the island. With a heavy heart, Ndétare bid his beloved goodbye; he gave her all his savings, enough to live on in the city before she found a job, no doubt as a maid. Sankèle went aboard, dressed as a man.

'You never know,' the boatman had said to his friend, 'we might run into fishermen. You'd better lend her one of your suits.'

And indeed, on the open sea, fishermen returning to the village waved at them enthusiastically, convinced they'd seen the schoolteacher. They were surprised to see him at the mosque early in the afternoon for Friday prayers.

'But we saw you leave early this morning, didn't we? You were in that boat they call *Saly Ndene*,' he heard them say.

'No,' he replied categorically, 'I was teaching this morning; ask the children. Anyway, as you know, I'm not allowed to leave the island, and I don't know how to sail a pirogue.'

Here, all boats have a name. Sometimes it's impossible to recognise the passengers, but pirogues are always identifiable by their speed, their flags and their individual paintwork. They had indeed seen *Saly Ndene* boldly cut through the waves. And as soon as the owner moored at the end of the day, he was asked about his companion. He swore he'd gone alone to Ndangane Sambou to buy spark plugs for *Saly Ndene*'s motor.

Express buses that left Ndangane Sambou in the morning tipped a crowd of villagers into the labyrinths of the capital city. Sankèle's little feet trod the black, filthy ground of Dakar. What became of her afterwards? No one ever knew.

Two years after these events, Niodior islanders returning from the city declared they'd seen her dancing in a ballet in the capital. Everyone was scandalised: a true *guelwaar* of noble descent doesn't put herself on show! Later, the waves flooded the village with another rumour: Sankèle had gone to practise her art in France. It was said the man from Barbès even tried to find her, but in vain. Lost in a nebulous elsewhere, Sankèle had become a vague shadow in an imaginary land. But for everyone here, France – El Dorado – also represented the furthest destination for every runaway and symbolised a kind of mythical place of perdition, the refuge for *Pitia-môme-Bopame*, the free birds who'd flown from every corner of the world. However, this last rumour had given some strength back to Sankèle's mother, who hoped to see her return from Europe one day with enough riches to restore the family's reputation. But time is the gravedigger of dreams. With the years, Sankèle's name no longer inspired stories or appeared in sorcerers' cowries. Only her mother and Ndétare had the shape of her slender silhouette engraved in their hearts. But she remained at the intersection of the lives of Ndétare, the old fisherman and the man from Barbès. Apparently separate, their destinies crossed and were linked in her. Rancour, anger, regret and frustration are merely the paths they borrowed to lead them to drink at the same well of memory. Of the three, Ndétare was the most affected by what had happened. Blinded by his convictions, the old fisherman remained persuaded that he had done what was necessary. As for the man from Barbès, his wound only itched in Ndétare's presence. The school-teacher alone had retained that painful fidelity which made new love impossible and regularly made him retreat into profound silence. In one of these phases, all the distractions he'd created to put his past behind him seemed suddenly ridiculous. Like Molière's *malade imaginaire*, he played the hypochondriac and unceremoniously dismissed the boys who came to pester him about football.

'I don't feel well, boys. We'll train another time. Anyway, it's not only physical exercise that counts; you must work your minds, too. You only think of looking after your bodies.'

'We love life! We want to keep ourselves in shape,' grumbled Garouwalé, the Poker, who always had to have the last word.

'Your being, your humanity, demands more than that. Learn to look outside yourselves. So use this free time to ask yourselves the real meaning of existence, that receding line. Is it possible to appreciate life when you've only yourself to love? And anyway, what's the point of running along the line when you know there's only a chasm at the end of it?'

The boys felt their shoulders sag under the weight of a cross that came from who knew where? At the time, Ndétare enjoyed the effect of his gloomy words. But as soon as the boys cleared off and he could hear only the echo of his walls, he prayed secretly that they'd come back to save him from those empty hours that dragged him towards the precipice.

8

MADICKÉ TOOK THE TEACHER'S WORDS literally and thought he'd found an answer. He wasn't self-centred, because he loved someone else more than he loved himself: Maldini. Everything he did was intended to bring him closer to him. Swayed by his friends and the old fisherman's jibes, he'd forgotten Ndétare's anti-emigration invectives.

The training sessions were the only outlet for Madické's frustration. And when there weren't any, idleness gave rise to the most unreasonable thoughts. So far, I'd managed to stop him from spending all his money, like his friends, on the marabouts who profited from the boys' innocent dreams. But this time he was adamant. He'd do anything to get to Europe to meet his idol, his double, and become a great footballer like him: that was his burning desire. And he would succeed, he was convinced of it.

'Hi! It's me, Madické.'

'Yes, hi. Are you OK?'

'Yes, phone me back at the call office.'

I hang up and call straight back. 'There's no match,' I say to myself. 'For him to call me in the middle of the day, something must have happened.'

'Right, go on, but make it quick. It's more expensive during the day.'

'Will you really help me come over?'

'Over where? I don't understand. You mean...'

'Yeah, to France. Help me find a club.'

'Are you crazy? I don't know anything about football. Anyway, how would I pay your fare? And more important: what would you live on?'

'Well, if you help me out with the ticket, it'll be fine. Afterwards, when I'm with a club, I'll earn—'

'Are you kidding? One, I can't afford to buy you a ticket, and, two, you'd be better off finding a decent club back home. There *are* a few, you know.'

'Yes, but I want to see Maldini play, and I won't get to see him by hanging around here.'

'Well, you won't see him in France either; he's Italian.'

'Yeah, OK, I know that! But the guys from here who leave for Italy usually go via France. You could help me out a little bit, couldn't you?'

'It's not that I don't want to, I just can't.'

'Fine, I'll go and see a marabout. At least they always know what to do.'

'Oh no! Don't you dare! You're not going to get ripped off by those swindlers. I forbid you to go!'

'Hold on a minute. You won't help me, so...I'll find a way all by myself.'

'But going to see a marabout isn't the answer to your problem! It's a load of old nonsense. How can you trust those people?'

'And why shouldn't I trust them? You're always putting them down, for no reason. But their powers have been proved time and time again. Look at Wagane; the village marabout helped him, and he made it. But you won't believe it; you think you learned everything there is to know at school! You're so westernised! And now Miss high-and-mighty criticises our customs. And worse: you've become an individualist, you won't even help me. So what makes you think you can tell me what I can and can't do?'

I hang up, slump on to the sofa and stare at the ceiling. Damn it, I can't tell my brother the sordid reasons why I run a mile from marabouts, can I?

To tell or not to tell? How do I tell him? Do I spell it out or not? So what do I do? A few lines appear on the ceiling. Narrator, your memory is a needle that weaves time into lace. And supposing the holes were more mysterious than the patterns you make? Which part of you could fill those holes? Who are you?

Metamorphosis! I am a leaf on a baobab tree, a coconut palm, a mango, quinqueliba, fégnéfégné or tabanany tree, I'm a wisp of straw. Not so, since the wind doesn't blow me away! Metamorphosis! I'm a block of this wall, a slab of marble, granite, a lump of onyx. I'm a bust by Rodin, a statue by Camille Claudel. Life passes me by and I'm this gap in the lattice of time. Not so, since my hand goes back and forth helping to weave time! A long time ago, in a little, dimly lit room, confronted with Africa and its rites, those thoughts were perhaps mine. Object they had made me, object I'd become.

Go on, Salie, continue! urged my guardian, old Coumba, facing her daughter, Gnarelle.

Coumba was well into her sixties, and her daughter had long turned thirty. I was at high school and had just moved to a different town to study, as many students did. My protective grandmother had insisted on placing me under the wing of a guardian angel, just until I found some kind of job and a small room to rent. After doing the rounds of her extended family, she'd entrusted me to Coumba, one of her cousins from the zillionth branch of the family tree. On the strength of our few shared genes, Coumba took me in. Thrilled mostly to get her hands on cheap labour, she kept me at her house for a long time, which was where I met her daughter, Gnarelle.

Living with her mother, Gnarelle was getting over a divorce. She showed off her two children to compensate for her demotion from the rank of wife. She was almost cured, for her attitude was once more triumphant and her smile suggestive. She was rediscovering the pleasures of seduction thanks to a wealthy fisherman, a neighbour of her mother's, who'd noticed her forced smile and seen through her make-up which signalled: *desperately hoping to get married again!*

When the young woman went down to the fishing port in the late afternoon, the former migrant worker Wagane Yaltigué, El Hadji with gold teeth who patrolled the shore checking the catches of his many pirogues, kept her firmly in view, watching her every move. He'd fill a plastic bucket with excellent-quality fish, slip in a large-denomination banknote and have it taken to her by a *môl*, an apprentice fisherman, who'd invariably say: 'Auntie, my uncle greets you and sends you some fish for your supper.'

It was a malodorous courtship, with no rose petals and an imagination that was flatter than a boat's hold, but it had the merit of being assiduous and well planned. Gnarelle would accept the offerings of fish, and eventually her forlorn heart became ardent. Her mother fanned the flames, urged on by others. Seemingly innocuous, the local griotte, romance's secret agent, who made her living by flattery, spread the rumours. When she dropped in to Coumba's to scrounge rice, money or soap, each time Gnarelle came into view she'd tease her: 'Ah, my girl! *Kar-Kar!* What can be said of such beauty, other than it melts the hearts of men, and no wonder. My dear Coumba, according to the folds in my *pagne*, the pirate who will capture our princess isn't far off: despite the grey hairs over his temples, he's handsome, he's kind and he gives money. A patina doesn't spoil quality wood; as we say in my native Baol, a man's beauty is in his pocket – which is also where the quivering lizard lies – but an old woman like me is no longer concerned with those things. Come, my girl, come and give your auntie griotte a few coins to buy a cola nut.' Without questioning her intuition, we'd give her a little money to get rid of her.

Shortly afterwards, in the house next door, the young woman grilled fish, which made El Hadji's taste buds tingle, and the aroma wafted over the wall and tickled mother Coumba's elderly nostrils. Serene now in her hovel, she relished the prospect of the captain and her own unhoped-for retirement. Every morning, imagining a future of filleted fish steak, she'd go, prayer beads in hand, and wish her saviour-son-in-law happy fishing. But the boss's best catch was definitely this nymph who gracefully stirred the breeze of the dying sun. He had made her his *gnarelle*, his second wife. Barely ten months after their wedding, she made him the proud father of a chubby baby, a boy. Gnarelle's husband and entire family of in-laws fêted her, lavished praise on her and showered her with gifts, so happy were they that their name was to be perpetuated.

Basking in adulation, Gnarelle became a splendid *dryanké*, a petulant, coquettish lady, with masses of jewellery and an enviable wardrobe. She sashayed across the large courtyard of the house and along the road to the market, and the swaying of her curvaceous hips mimicked the pitching of the pirogues on the waves of the Atlantic.

All this went on in front of Simâne, the first wife, who had withdrawn into her own orbit to distance herself from this orgy of joy. But she couldn't help eavesdropping, and amid the congratulations showered on her petulant co-spouse she overheard various spiteful proverbs and gibes directed at herself, for she'd never borne her husband anything but daughters.

People called her 'the broken calabash', unable to contain the future, her seven children being only pieces of herself: nothing but girls! People also said that, because of her, her husband had to feed useless mouths that would only go to swell another man's family instead of helping perpetuate the name of Yaltigué.

Simâne fretted in her bedroom, accompanied by sadness and solitude, her only remaining friends. She'd throw her arms in the air, repeating sayings that had been sown in her brain and which tangled together like weeds: 'Feeding girls is like fattening cows that will never produce any milk.' Or: 'A herdsman without a bull will end up with no herd.'

She recalled the taunts that had plagued her husband before his marriage to Gnarelle. El Hadji Wagane Yaltigué spent a lot of time in the local square, which was packed with men – his neighbours and fellow fishermen – whose wealth was evident in their many wives flanked by armies of scrawny kids. They all considered El Hadji's monogamy shameful. Behind his back they called him one-ball, because men with two balls ought to have at least two wives. Some said that the only thing El Hadji was capable of taking was the sea, that at home it was Simâne who wore the trousers, which was why he didn't dare take a second wife. Others said that he was monogamous to copy the whites, for he'd lived in France a long time. Well-meaning souls had pointed out to El Hadji that he needed to enhance his status, and had offered their services to remedy the situation. They were keen to remind him that he still didn't have a male child. Seven being the magic number, they concluded that when a woman doesn't give satisfaction after that many births, there's nothing more to hope for from her.

'Those servants of Satan have ruined my life! Let them all rot in hell!'

And Simâne's monologue would culminate in an

outburst of anger: 'And now a stuck-up little nobody, married twenty-five years after me, gives my husband the bull he'd been wanting for so long! Cursed be my belly, which has borne me nothing but misery!'

Confined to her hell, Simâne kept her raging hormones in check with erotic fantasies and memories of embraces, embraces that no longer took place except in her tactile memory – and in another part of the building, where Gnarelle graciously allowed herself to be taken. From the depths of her emotional isolation, Simâne watched the young, already established reign of Gnarelle, whose luck and love she envied, until the day…

Gnarelle delighted in her matrimonial throne; she took pleasure in her position and did everything she could to maintain it. She wanted to contain the passions of her Hadji within the boundaries of her triangle, but it would require more than the gurgling of a baby. So she varied the dishes she set down before her husband, her hairstyles and the little attentions she paid him. When evening came, the lace trimmings on her lingerie offered glimpses of the many facets of her sensuality. *Allah Akbar*, El Hadji would say, pretending to avert his eyes when, on his way to the mosque for evening prayer, he bumped into her on the steps or in the courtyard. It was lucky he always wore baggy trousers! *Allah Akbar!* God is great! Gnarelle was radiant, oblivious to the sighs of El Hadji's first wife, until the day…

Until the day she needed some ginger to perk up the sauces and cocktails she was concocting for her husband, and much more besides. But neither ginger nor her lingerie, which had gradually become more garish and transparent, were enough to get things back on an even keel and restore her greying husband's appetite for love. The sun had finally set, and the quivering lizard had deserted its refuge. Would they return tomorrow? Perhaps, if it doesn't rain and if the lizard doesn't find a better sanctuary!

Despite the prayers and incense, Gnarelle's tomorrows were rainy, and the lizard did not seek out its refuge. In the morning she rose, gloomy, from a bed whose sheets were barely creased. She eventually fell asleep, her passion unquenched; her Hadji, whom she thought grown feeble, was satisfying his passion elsewhere and seemed to be developing a taste for it.

An elderly farmer from Fimela, who'd long owed him a lot of money, had just offered him his sixteen-year-old daughter's hand. Who said barter had died out in modern Africa? The old farmer thus wiped out his debt and at the same time forged an enviable alliance. And although El Hadji hadn't asked for anything, he didn't exactly object. I've never known a lion turn its nose up at a gazelle. El Hadji stayed in Fimela for many long months.

Tired of watching and waiting, Gnarelle went to cry on her mother's shoulder. Coumba, a woman of experience, resolved to remedy her daughter's unhappiness straightaway. They must entice the wayward husband back and keep him, and they'd stop at nothing for such an important cause. After making all the requisite sacrifices to invoke the memory of the ancestors, in vain, mother Coumba called in a Peul marabout whose reputation had spread through the city of M'Bour like a trail of paprika. Here, we like our food hot, and the rumours at the market make the mouth water, whetting the appetites of women who have no idea how to spice up their stale relationships. The polygamy match is never played without marabouts. In this instance, *marabout* – that ancient-sounding, round, sonorous, plump word – took the form of a young man who reeked of eau de Cologne and whose demeanour suggested an out-and-out womaniser. He turned up at mother Coumba's one evening, respecting the tacit code of discretion which dictates that in this society, where many people won't even go to the toilet without consulting their marabout, no one openly admits to having one.

And so the surgeon who was to patch up Gnarelle's broken heart, iron out her crumpled relationship and give her a second youth arrived one evening with a huge bag as his only luggage. My guardian, mother Coumba, commanded me to vacate my room, where she was to receive the Peul. It was a small, scantily furnished room that had served as a storeroom before my arrival. A prayer mat and a kettle had been placed there for the holy guest's ablutions. After his first evening prayer, I was given the job of serving him a succulent dinner in a good-sized bowl, a whole melon, sweetened curds and a bottle of well-chilled lemonade. Coumba and her daughter respected *téranga*, national hospitality, and were well-versed in *téralgane* – the art of entertaining a guest in style.

However, while that old mosquito El Hadji had been sucking the blood of the little Fimela girl and injecting her with his seed, he'd infected her with that malaria of the city, an immoderate taste for the bourgeois life. Associating changes in her body with those of her social situation, the little country girl became increasingly ardent in her desire to consume old wood. Back in M'Bour, Simâne, the first wife, depended on nocturnal food deliveries from her relatives, and Gnarelle was getting deeper and deeper into debt in order to keep up appearances. Meanwhile, back in Fimela, El Hadji was allowing himself to be caught in a younger, therefore stronger, net. To hold on to him, the girl would claim she was suffering fever and giddiness, which owed nothing to love but which he chose to interpret as the effects of Cupid's arrows – either from naivety or a deliberate ignorance of the difference between a sigh of vexation and an orgasmic moan. While Gnarelle sought to conceal her sadness beneath the cold sand of the M'Bour nights, his new ladylove was desperately trying to feign passion – which was even more exhausting.

After dinner, old Coumba called her daughter. They both told the marabout the cause of their worries and the miracle they expected of him. The Peul enumerated his successes, giving a list of women's first names, a whole host of satisfied customers. To conclude the consultation, he looked up and turned his palms heavenwards, his clear voice filling the room with 'bismillah', followed by a string of words that were unintelligible to the two women. In a reverent silence, they imitated his gesture, except that they didn't reach up towards the sky but towards their intercessor, who, at the end of his prayer, sprayed them with a jet of holy saliva. *Alhamdoulilah!* Thanks be to Allah! Gnarelle and her mother, in awe of the tall young man and his grigris, withdrew, bowing in reverence and filled with hope. Now the holy man wished to be left alone to pray and meditate before going to bed - for, he said, it was during the night that he talked to the spirits and received their instructions. Naturally these spirits determined the price of his services, a necessary recompense.

Gradually the town's voice died away. I set up my temporary bed in the sitting room. The night of spirits descended in her long black robe, clouding minds and obscuring the line of Cartesian thinking, snuffing out the flames that Mariama Bâ, Ousmane Sembène and others had struggled to kindle. The truth was still waiting for Godot! My sleep, too. When everyone was in bed, the Peul walked through the sitting room to go to the toilet. Well, well! Could he be a man like any other? Marabouts are supposed to find solutions to everything, and I imagined they'd worked out, for themselves at least, a way of dealing with those little calls of nature so inconvenient for meditation. But this marabout at any rate was able to postpone his needs. I watched him warily through half-shut eyes. He'd paused by my makeshift bed and was staring at me. But nature called, urging him to go. And when he came back? Metamorphosis! I am a tarnished bronze Buddha, souls emerge from Lucifer's cave, leave me their shadows and vanish, haloed in my light. Buddha, I hold my breath when, swept along by the river of sins, piercing eyes sink their blades into my mute, passive flesh. On his return, then, the marabout stood still beside my bed and, his mouth half-open, gazed at me for a long time. '*Youmam Babam, Allahou Akbar!*' he murmured before moving off. Had the spirits inspired a plan of action? Had they made my body the parchment of a secret letter?

The following morning, in front of his quinqueliba tea, half a baguette with plenty of butter and some piping-hot home-made doughnuts, he greeted my guardian and her daughter, who'd arrived at the first cockcrow. In a long ascending speech, he revealed the procedure for restoring Gnarelle's happiness. Handing the young woman a cord interwoven with young roots, a mixture of crushed herbs and a bottle filled with a dark liquid, he explained: 'From now on you will wear this cord around your waist. Put three pinches of this powder in your husband's food every evening for a week. Start on a Friday and finish the following Friday.'

Gnarelle, her head bowed, reverently held her hands out to 'the lord', chanting her gratitude.

'This bottle,' the Peul went on, 'be careful with the liquid inside, it contains a very powerful spell. If your husband's other wives are affected by it, it will inevitably backfire on you. Beware of the other wives, and I stress this, for they operate in the shadows.'

'*Wallaye, wallaye!*' cried mother Coumba. 'My daughter has become passive, it's as if she's been drained of all her energy.'

Then, looking at him through tear-filled eyes, the old

woman added: 'I knew they weren't harmless.'

'*Deugue, deugue,* truly,' murmured Gnarelle, 'my body no longer obeys me and I don't sleep a wink all night. I'm sure they've put a curse on me.'

'Don't worry,' continued the dashing marabout, his face illuminated with a smile. 'God gives us the answer to each of our worries. *Insh'Allah*, everything will return to normal if you follow my instructions to the letter.'

'We will do everything you tell us,' chorused the two women.

Then, to confirm their total submission, mother Coumba drew on a proverb, as if rubber-stamping an official declaration: 'When you don't know the way, you follow in the guide's footsteps.'

'It's not up to me to tell you what to do. I only convey to you what the spirits command,' explained the Peul. 'The spirits can resolve your problem, but it's up to you to earn their benevolence by following their instructions to the letter.'

'*Wallaye, wallaye,*' the old woman acquiesced humbly, protected by the wall of her proverb.

The master went on with his duties.

'And so, I was telling you to be very careful with the liquid in this bottle,' he said, turning his light-skinned face towards Gnarelle. 'To use it, add a little perfume. Then, when you spend the night with your husband, anoint yourself with this liquid before joining him in bed. Most important, you must dab it on your private parts three times, calling out his name, and, *insh'Allah*, he won't be able to resist you.'

The young woman lapped up his words. Her eyes had already found their old sparkle again as they followed the thread of a dream.

'But that is not all.' Now the Peul snapped the dream's thread: 'Give me fifty thousand CFA francs, two lengths of blue cotton and a young sheep or the equivalent in cash, for I must make sacrifices to the spirits for their service to you. Of course, I'm not the one who determines the nature or the value of these material things; it's the spirits who demand them. They're invisible to the ordinary mortal, but all the same they're just like us, they have their little whims. The worst is that they have no qualms about taking their revenge on the children of those who fail to fulfil their demands.'

'It will be done, their wishes will be satisfied,' the two women solemnly promised.

'In addition,' went on the marabout, 'there's a further ritual which is rather special, and I'll understand if you say no. Let me just add that it's a ritual that I offer my best clients free of charge, to help them, to guarantee the complete success of the work we've begun. The decision is yours, ladies...'

Despite the obscurity of this clause, the two women agreed with alacrity. If you're dying of thirst in the desert you don't stop a stone's throw from the oasis! The same day, at the time for midday prayer – the moment when the magic powers are at full strength, according to the marabout – the ritual was carried out.

The Peul's ritual required a pure young girl, a virgin, to hold the maraboutal penis and move her hand up and down, from the ground to the sky and from the sky to the ground, with a motion like pounding millet, while he lay on his back between his patient's legs, chanting his incantations. Coumba, my guardian, had seized and gagged me, telling me of the terrible fate that awaited me, the horrendous punishment the spirits would inflict on me if I refused or gave away the secret. The marabout supported her, saying: 'The belly is noble: it is a tomb for secrets, and whoever opens that tomb must put up with the stench. When I walk through the forest, I avoid trampling on useful plants, but I tear off branches that are in my way,' he said, looking in my direction, silencing me with his eyes.

In the gloom of the little room, a thin shaft of light poked through the curtain and intermittently lit up Gnarelle's and her mother Coumba's faces. A voice inside me repeated frenziedly: I am an ebony statue, but God commands me to breathe; my chest rises spasmodically. Help, I am alive. God commands me to breathe! And I breathed, despite myself.

'Go, on, Salie. Continue, I say!' commands old Coumba.

I imagined I was somewhere else: I'm an automaton, her voice is a wind blowing around me and doesn't affect my rhythmic movements.

'Well, get on with it!' shrieked the old woman. 'For goodness' sake, Salie, go on, faster than that! *Athia! Athia waaye!*'

'Salie, *athia waaye*,' echoed Gnarelle, out of loyalty to her mother.

Metamorphosis! I'm a sandcastle. Let an Atlantic wave wash over me! A ball of mud, a billiard ball, a bubble of life, I am a low-pressure zone. The cyclone of their voices shook me, my hand was shaking, the sliding, up-and-down movement somehow accelerated. Faster, eyes closed; faster, looking away; faster still, biting my lips; even faster, my hand, damp at first, became sticky; faster, my orifices beseech God for valves, my being must be sealed. Faster! They still urged, filling the room with their voices. One day, for sure, I'll make them drink my molten brain, faster than that! But who am I?

Metamorphosis! I am a grigri. I am a magic potion. I am a length of blue cotton fabric. I am that young sheep, its throat slit on the altar of Gnarelle's love. I am a sacrifice to the spirits. I am one of the Peul marabout's charms. That's why my hand was sliding non-stop up and down that thing I was afraid to look at.

As soon as the marabout's member pointed to the

heavens, Gnarelle was instructed to lie on her back, her feet and arms outstretched. She was also to clutch a grigri in each hand and to press down on a third with her hips. We had reached this stage when the marabout let out a sigh and signalled for the sacrifice to stop. The beast's head was pointing to the roof of the little room; my hand felt as if it had been squeezing okra. The Peul turned around, recited a prayer and, chanting other cryptic words, straddled Gnarelle, who went rigid on the mat.

'Don't worry,' he said, 'I'm just introducing the positive fluid.'

Gnarelle was absolutely still. She clutched her grigris tightly. It was so long since she'd clenched her fists in this position. Old Coumba rose and led me out of the little room, murmuring: '*Alhamdoulilah*, that's the last phase of the ritual. Come, the wise man doesn't need us any more, but whatever you do, don't go telling a soul about this, otherwise you'll die a cruel and violent death for certain.'

Some time had elapsed since the marabout's departure. the Fimela girl's little belly had prompted El Hadji and his third wife to move closer to M'Bour hospital. Three months after the Peul's ritual, El Hadji returned and spent two nights with each of his wives in turn. The seventh night of the week was the bonus reserved for his young third wife. The Peul's potion had worked, but Gnarelle's privileges had still not been reinstated and she remained a secondary wife. Six months after her husband's return, she gave birth to a healthy baby. However, he was less chubby and much lighter-skinned than his elder brother. Rumours flew. But since it was a boy, El Hadji legally recognised him as being of the Yaltigué lineage. Thus he gained a second son and Gnarelle's total submission, now that she was bound to him by shame and gratitude for so generously giving his name to the fair-skinned child.

Meanwhile, I'd become resistant to any form of guardian-
ship during my wanderings. I made my memory a tomb for
this story for many long years. I only exhumed it to show
Madické what many marabouts conceal beneath their saintly
appearance. No, it wasn't fear that was stopping me, but
rather decency; for it didn't take me long to realise that the
Peul marabout's sole power consisted of his ability to
propagate his genes wherever the wind blew, and that the
spirits he invoked resided in his trousers.

When I finally told him this story, Madické muttered: 'So
what? God alone will be the judge. Not all of them are like
that one. Marabouts have always settled problems in Africa.
And anyway, every soul is a labyrinth: people find help
wherever they can!'

Deeply rooted in his culture, he still had absolute faith in
ancestral practices. According to him, you had to try them all
before admitting defeat. Each time we spoke, I tried to
dissuade him. Irritated by my constant nagging, Madické,
who seemed to be simmering with anger, eventually came
out with it: 'Seeing as you won't help me, let me do things my
way. You've turned into a European, an individualist. A guy
from the village who's back from France says you're doing
very well over there, that you've published a book. He swears
he's even seen you on TV. People say a newspaper from here
has written things about your book too. So with all the
money you're making, you'd have paid my fare and brought
me over to live with you if you weren't so selfish.'

So that's why my brother had itchy feet. The man who'd
reported this news had built up his hopes. The multi-million-
aire football stars he worshipped were on TV. No doubt in his
mind: his sister, seen on TV, especially in France, must have
become rich. Of course, you don't have to live in the third
world to fall under the spell of the media.

Madické's informer – a labourer who went from one

temporary job to another – knew nothing of life in France apart from the din of factories, the insides of sewers and the ratio of dog shit per square of pavement. Holed up in a tiny cell in a Sonacotra hostel for immigrants with one of his wives, his European food wouldn't make a Niodior fisherman's mouth water. A stock of provisions, the bare minimum, constantly replenished depending on special offers, enabled him to stash the bulk of his earnings under his mattress. Careful management of his meagre resources had permitted what, in his eyes, represented the height of luxury: a wife in France, smuggled in, to feed the hard worker; another to greet him in Dakar, a haven for the warrior's well-earned rest; and a third among the mangroves on the island, to keep him in touch with his roots. As soon as winter knocked at the city's doors, he'd pack his bags; that season and monogamy were two of the few things he didn't envy the French. He wished he could take everything back with him: his shopping list began at Roissy the minute he arrived and ended at Roissy, the day of his departure. His list was exhaustive: from a suit to Y-fronts, not forgetting an electric shaver, of no use in the village, and even an atomiser, which soon turned into plain warm rain beneath the coconut palms; he omitted nothing. Anxious to curry favour with his ladies, he bought them essential toiletries, imitating women shoppers in his choice of products, as well as the heavy household appliances that he bought second-hand. He'd even taken a dozen pairs of gloves for his ladylove on the island, to prevent her hands being blistered by the pestle. But she hardly wore them; after briefly trying them on, she'd flung them onto the roof of the chicken run. The thought was sweet, but it took more than a bit of plastic France to satisfy her.

No, what she wanted was to fly over the Atlantic, to settle on the other side and watch TV every night beside her husband. She wanted her children, like those of the first wife, to be able to say: I was born in Fraaance! So her darling husband could give the gloves to the matronly woman who delivered her of a baby every year in the mud, on a pile of empty potato sacks that served as a birthing table. Her husband had promised to take her there, but she'd given up hoping ten years ago. In the second year of her marriage she'd received a letter from him that had led her to believe he was taking care of the formalities so she might join him, that he was saving up to pay her fare and even that he was looking for a bigger apartment. Overjoyed, she had spent all her savings on making preparations. She generously gave away all her pots and pans as well as the little furniture she had, and shared out her wardrobe among her sisters and cousins, keeping for herself only her few western outfits, before bidding goodbye to the admiring villagers and going to Dakar-Yoff to await her departure. After four patient months, she returned to the village with stooped shoulders, her braids frayed and henna faded. After the questioning came the gibes. There's no way to block your ears, and she heard everything but said little, and barely showed her eyes, which were sinking deep into their sockets. At the spectacle of her impoverishment, everyone who'd benefited from her generosity tacitly agreed to return what she'd given them. With no gloves or balm, she took back pestle and mortar and vented her fury pounding the millet. The thumping sound felt like a betrayal. Worse still, she could hear Satan sniggering. Her husband, meanwhile, was dreading the trip home, but it took more than this to persuade him to spend a winter in France. Rather than make do with over-spiced sauces by way of heating, he set off to top up his tan and live a temporary life of ease in the tropics. A jobber left the anonymous immigrants' hostel but a pharaoh landed in Dakar, on his way to set up court in the village. During these trips, he felt all his sacrifices were justified and acceptable,

but even so, they obsessed him. No matter how hard he tried
to forget them, they came back intact and threatening, as the
time for him to return to France drew near. Surrounded by
his family and childhood friends, he was distressed at the
idea of returning to the immense solitude that awaited him.

Over there, a merciless lucidity acquired over time had
made him distance himself from the friendships he'd built up
during the days of his Banania grin. A newcomer, desperate
for human warmth and unaware of the cost of living, he
entertained as he did at home. On Sundays, despite the
cramped conditions he lived in, he'd invite colleagues of
different nationalities to sit at his table where, to honour him,
his wife would serve *thiéboudjène* or copious helpings of
chicken *yassa*. At the café, he always offered to buy a round.
But the difficulties of finding temporary work and trying to
make ends meet had made him bitter, particularly since none
of these French friends seemed keen to introduce him to the
local specialities. Disappointed, he went out less and spent
his money sparingly. He didn't miss his colleagues, whom
he'd originally thought of as friends. The whites he said he
couldn't stand, because of their insidious way of putting
racism into perspective the better to practise it, remaining
oblivious to the difficulties of those who are its victims. The
blacks he couldn't stand any longer, because of their
insistence on seeing racism everywhere, especially those
losers who wouldn't even have made a go of fly-fishing back
home. A radical anti-racist, he himself had become racist, he
declared, he was *anti-moron*, irrespective of race.

In France, apart from Youssou N'Dour CDs, which he
listened to non-stop, and morose-rose dinners with his
devoted wife, he relied on the TV for entertainment. Just
imagine, then, his excitement when he happened to switch
on and see this distant cousin, whose address he didn't even
know, on the screen. For the first time in his life, he watched

a literary programme all the way through. He was familiar only with the cover of her book, but that was enough to embroider it into a saga which he was impatient to relate the minute he was back in the village. Who would dare hold it against him? Pride in one's identity is the exiles' dopamine. And then, giving news of a fellow migrant to their family back home always earns you gratitude and admiration. So, just as nursing auxiliaries boost their image by passing themselves off as doctors, supply teachers as lecturers, cleaning operatives as hotel managers, some of those returning on holiday report in great detail the lives of people they know nothing about. Thus, Mr Sonacotra basked in my brother's credulity just as he did in the sun.

9

IN NIODIOR, THE MAN FROM Barbès' stories followed the trail of imagination, capturing the hearts of the young islanders. Like his friends, Madické was single-minded, and he firmly believed I could help make his dream come true. He had only one thought in his head: to leave, go far away, flying over the black land to touch down in the white land that burns with a thousand lights. To leave, and not look back. You don't look back when you're walking on the tightrope of a dream. Go to see that grass where the last drops of the Atlantic run dry, which is said to be so much greener, *over there,* where the local authorities pay people who clean up dog shit, *over there,* where even those who don't work get a wage. Go to that place where foetuses already have bank accounts in their names, and babies have career plans. And cursed were those who took it upon themselves to thwart the wishes of the young islanders.

I'd had this unfortunate experience myself, during a summer holiday in the village a few months before the European Cup. My brother was dead set on leaving the country. From his earliest childhood, his mind had been contaminated by the older boys. He'd grown up with the notion of leaving, of success to be found elsewhere, at any price; over the years it had become his destiny. Emigration was the clay out of which he planned to model his future, his entire life.

The urge to return to the source is irresistible, for it's reassuring to think that life is easier to grasp in the place where it puts down its roots. And yet, for me, returning is the same as leaving. I go home as a tourist in my own country, for I have become the *other* for the people I continue to call my family. I no longer know how to interpret the excitement caused by my arrival. Are these people who crowd around me coming to celebrate someone from their community, to squeeze some money out of me, to find out about foreign parts that fascinate them, or are they simply here to inspect and judge the curious creature I've perhaps become in their eyes?

By the day after my arrival, the bundles of firewood had burned out, leaving the smoke to accompany the prayers heavenwards. An army of feathered creatures, fattened for other occasions, had expired under the blade of the knife, which will plead not guilty at the Last Judgment. The huge ceremonial cooking pots had fulfilled their purpose, the women their duties, and the men had filled their bellies. The lunch was lavish and everyone had a feast. God puts food in each mouth He creates: that day, the proverb held true. Some, like the old fisherman, seemed to have come to make up for their various nutritional deficiencies. Nobody asked my opinion; I was simply informed how much it cost to provide a slap-up meal for all these people, who'd invited themselves. The community ethos prevails over good manners, or rather, it underpins them. We must share everything, our joys as well as our sorrows. The collective memory keeps trotting out the old adage: what belongs to each, belongs to all. I know this social rule is profoundly humane, but when it's abused it mostly benefits the lazy while maintaining them in a state of chronic dependence. I was supposed to feed these self-invited guests without batting an eyelid, for fear of being seen as a western individualist, an unnaturally selfish person, from the moment I arrived. As for the few people with reservations, islanders living in the city and new recruits to modern society, they soon resorted to genealogy to justify their presence. But everybody knew the crowning argument: 'She's come from France,' they'd say, and the general implication of this little phrase was more eloquent than any speech. Budgeted to last a month, my spending money, a meagre sum I'd struggled to earn, was trickling through my fingers. What can you do? People who can't afford a leg of lamb are glad of the carcass. Dare to tell them they've got a nerve and they'll send you packing, using in their defence the crowning argument that the worst outrage of the twenty-first century is the west growing obese while the third world starves. My savings were my body of Christ, my suffering turned into cake for my folks. Here, eat, brothers, this is my sweat, sold in Europe for you! Hosanna!

After lunch, the boys of the house, soon joined by their friends, gathered in the sitting room for tea. Madické was there with Garouwalé, his best friend, actually one of our distant cousins; here, friendships often mirror blood ties. Garouwalé never missed tea-time. Quite the connoisseur, he was reputed to be the group's best tea-maker. His friends were unanimous in assigning him the job. At first, he pretended to say no, then let them implore him, enjoying seeing his skills recognised and in demand, before gladly accepting. Acting all high and mighty, he gave the most thankless task to the youngest boy, who grumbled a bit before obeying. His job was to bring the equipment and fetch charcoal and paper to light the stove. As if used to being a servant, he discovered a clever trick: in the kitchen, the wood that had been used to cook the lunch was still burning. He took away the stove and brought it back full of smouldering embers. I watched the boys' little game with Ndétare, who'd come to see me, and we exchanged censorious looks, making asides in French.

'The older boys aren't prepared to give up their privileges,' I said. 'The youngest obey, praying that time will speed up.'

'Yes!' he replied in the tone of a well-informed ethnologist. 'The same kids who complain today that this prerogative is unfair will be abusing it in their turn in the name of tradition.'

The skivvy for the day carried out his duties. On a tray a dozen tarnished cups were draining; a bunch of mint sat infusing in a small calabash and was already filling the sitting room with its fragrance. The tea ceremony could begin. The master felt the weight of the packets of tea and sugar, darted a knowing look at Madické, who gave a brief nod in my direction, and they broke into happy childish laughter that made me smile, too. This midday break gave them the chance to discuss all sorts of things. Even when I was away, Ndétare liked to invite himself to join the boys; it was a ready-made opportunity for him to continue his educational mission.

'It's good you come back and visit us from time to time,' he said to me. 'I see you haven't changed. You've grown, but you're still the tomboy of the family ; you still steer clear of women's gossip. I've always known you'd get away from all this back-biting, but I'm pleased to see the little liana has deep roots.'

I was the only girl to be found behind the boys' closed doors, as I had been before I left. The women were clustered in the kitchen and already thinking about the dish they'd be cooking for dinner. We could hear muffled bursts of laughter and the clatter of pots and pans. Cut off from the rest of the household and accustomed to domestic duties from early childhood, they went about their business without really thinking about it.

Here, the kitchen's a living place that takes up a lot of room. A third of the house is shut off, reserved for culinary activities: this is the women's preserve. While they work solely to delight the palate, their conversation revolves around the harvests, the fishermen's meagre catch, the shellfish they have to go further and further to find, weddings and baptisms, fabrics that are in fashion and new styles. Practising sublime alchemy, they can conquer the onion's arrogance, garlic's temerity and chilli's fire to restore a dash of character to a swordfish tamed by sizzling oil. They patiently blend tomatoes and potatoes in a finely orches-trated ballet. But above all they're magicians, transforming grains of rice into rubies, simply by asking the palm tree to bestow on them the goodness it has drawn from the earth and the sun. Busy as they were, they paid attention to the men's chat that went on *mezza voce* in the adjoining courtyard. The words reached them, borne on a breath of desire that boldly slipped beneath their *pagnes*.

The women didn't often invite me into their world, nor did I participate much in their activities. They scarcely involved me in the preparations to celebrate my return, other than to ask me to pay. I didn't go with them to chop wood for the fire; they hadn't called me when they left at dawn. I'd heard them, but hadn't got out of bed. They knew I wouldn't have wanted to go, and I knew they wouldn't have wanted me with them. It was a tacit agreement. My presence made them uncomfortable. They had long considered me a lazybones who couldn't do anything with her ten fingers other than turn the pages of a book, a self-centred person who preferred to shut herself away to scribble than to take part in conversations in the garden outside the kitchen. During the excitement of the preparations, they'd watch me pacing from one corner to another or writing, and it would irritate them. I could read the reproach under their black eyelashes, but my silence disarmed them; they pretended to ignore me. My pen went on tracing the path I'd taken to leave them. Every notebook I filled, every book I read, every dictionary I consulted was one more brick in the wall dividing us. And yet, unwittingly, they encouraged my solitary activity. You don't hurl yourself into folded arms: their disdain exempted me from all formality. Even if you're starved of affection, you don't go kissing sea urchins.

In the village I'm sometimes glad people ignore me; it's one way to be left in peace. The traditional community is of course a great comfort, but it drags you down and smothers you. It's a steamroller that crushes you, the better to absorb you. The ties that bind the individual to the group are so stifling you think only of breaking them. True, the fields of duty and entitlement are adjacent, but the snag is that the former's so vast that you spend your entire life ploughing it, and you attain the latter only when old age makes freedom redundant. The sense of belonging is a private feeling that's taken for granted; to impose it on others is to deny their ability to define themselves freely. But go tell that to the diehards who believe the herd is the only thing worthwhile! They'll beat the whitey individualist out of you and marginalise you. When this judgment comes down on your head, it's the women who are most vindictive. Their smug sarcasm distils acid into your blood, the rolling of their eyes sends you into orbit, and their fluttering eyelashes crack like a whip, banishing you from their good graces. It was to avoid them, or rather because I was tired of having to explain and defend myself, that I preferred the company of boys; in that respect, they were less hostile. In any case, macho from birth, they weren't at all shocked by the fact that I went against the women's will, even if those women were their mothers.

However, they did think it was acceptable to impose theirs on me, unaware that the thirst for freedom pays little heed to the oppressor's sex.

From time to time, Garouwalé, who was making the tea, went to serve the men under the palaver tree and then the women, who greeted him with saucy innuendo. He could have given the job to another boy, but this way he could parade in front of the girls, who acted all innocent in front of their mothers, always on the lookout for an improbable wealthy son-in-law. Garouwalé would come back from the ladies' court with a smile on his face and instantly throw himself into the conversation. Each time, Madické or someone else in the room would sum up what had been said in his absence.

The afternoon was already flagging, human shadows lengthened eastwards for the rest of this torrid day. Garouwalé took his time. In these parts you always know when tea begins, but never when it ends. A nice rest for the workers, but also, some might say, the perfect tranquilliser to cosset the unemployed and allow them to forget their desperate situation. During this idle interlude, when life seems to slow down as you digest, we'd reached the tea of love.

Tea, known here as *attaya*, has three tasting stages, each preceded by a lengthy preparation. For the first, the tea is very strong, with little sugar. The infusion is served piping hot and very bitter. It's hard to swallow and only those who are used to it can take it; we call it the tea of death. During the second phase, which is sweeter, the tea is weaker and mint is added, which makes it very pleasant to sip. As sweet as the saliva of a first kiss, the palate is excited by it; it is the tea of love. But, alas! This pleasure is fleeting and followed by a kind of nostalgia: the third and last serving, a very sugary, yellowish liquid, which now contains only the memory of tea, is the tea of friendship.

Garouwalé had just returned from serving the second round when Madické summed up what I'd said with the following words: 'She says we shouldn't go to France!'

'I didn't say that,' I corrected him. 'I said you shouldn't go there under any conditions.'

'Explain what you mean, sis,' commanded Garouwalé.

'I mean, I don't think you should just go there and leave things to chance.'

'So how d'you want us to go?' asked Madické. 'Maybe we should wait for Chirac to come and meet us at the airport?'

Ndétare stared wide-eyed: he'd just realised that Madické, the one he thought was the most sensible, the only one he believed he'd discouraged from wanting to leave, was in no less a hurry to pack his bags than the rest of them. He'd always said, 'You should sow ideas wherever they're likely to grow,' and had sown his relentlessly, but now he saw to his dismay that the Atlantic had irrigated and killed off his crop. Here, in the salt marshes, everyone's prepared to go and seek their share of sugar cane elsewhere. And each crystal of salt shines with that hope.

'Tell them,' begged the schoolteacher. 'Tell them! You live over there. Maybe they'll listen to you; they think I'm just a crazy old fool. They used to swear they wanted to go over there to play football for the big clubs; they didn't fool me, but I often made excuses for them, since their words still contained a little fragment of a dream, of poetry. Now, I no longer have any doubt: they're simply blinded by unbridled greed, even though, like the rest of us, they listen to the news in their own language and hear reports on the problems our people have over there. But there's nothing you can do about it; they're ready to risk their skin for even a rabbit hutch in France. Go on, tell them they're unable to behold the beam that is in their own eye. Tell them all the things you told me the other day.'

'Don't be stupid!' I told my brother, trying to keep it short. 'You know very well what I mean. You mustn't go there with nothing, illegally, it's suicide. It's not the good Lord's house. You don't parachute in as if it's a field of millet – in any case, not as easily as you think.'

'Hey, guys! Just listen to big sis,' sneered Garouwalé, the Poker. 'Now she's there, now she's made a packet, she's closing the door. She's saying all that so she doesn't have to put us up.'

'I'm not trying to stop you but to warn you. If you turn up without any papers, you're going to run into serious problems and have a miserable existence in France.'

'Hey, we're hard workers, we are! Aren't we, guys?' said Madické, needlessly urging on his allies, who were already on a war footing. 'We're capable of finding jobs and holding on to them like real men. You managed it, and you're only a girl. There are old men now living a cushy life in the village – they succeeded over there, so why shouldn't we?'

'You're wrong. In the past, just after the Second World War, the French welcomed lots of people with open arms because they needed workers to rebuild the country. They hired immigrants from all over the place who agreed to go and risk their lives down the coal mines to escape poverty. Many of those people have contributed to pensions they'll never draw. Very few really did make a go of things. Successive waves of African immigrants have all ended up in slums. They dream nostalgically of an unlikely return to their homeland, a land which, to be honest, worries them more than it attracts them because it's changed while they've been away, and when they do go back for their rare holidays they feel like foreigners. Their children, who've grown up with the refrain "Liberty, Equality, Fraternity", no longer have any illusions once they realise, after a long battle, that their hard-won naturalisation doesn't improve their opportunities. Proof of nationality isn't stamped on your forehead! Unless they make chadors from Joan of Arc's flag, they have no way of convincing the colour-prejudiced of their tricolour identity. In Europe, my brothers, you're black first, citizens incidentally, outsiders permanently, and that's certainly not written in the constitution, but some can read it on your skin. So, you see, it's not enough just to set foot on French soil in order to live the life of those minimum-wage tourists who make you drool when they dump their cheap trash *Made in Paradise* on you. There's unemployment over there now, too. What assets do you have that'll guarantee you success over there? When you're ambitious, you need a broad back. As illegal immigrants with no qualifications, you'll find it a hard slog if you're lucky enough not to get picked up by the police, who'll bundle you onto the next plane home.'

'Exactly!' said Ndétare, in raptures. 'Listen carefully, because you're blinkered. Now you see I wasn't over-dramatising. I know cows in Normandy are fat, but that doesn't make it a rich pasture for stray sheep! Look out for the thorns, boys. Be careful!'

'That's a bit of an exaggeration,' retorted the brains of the gang, who'd just been expelled from school because he had to repeat the year too many times. 'I know a couple of guys in the town where I was studying: they left two years ago and they're still there; they haven't been sent back even though they only have tourist visas. And my friend Samba, their little brother, is going over to join them soon. It's definitely not as hard as you make out. Look at all the foreigners who play in their national team. Besides, at the moment, the Prime Minister's a socialist, like Senghor; the left's in power, and they're the ones who're supposed to help the poor, right?'

'Except that, over there, no one notices the poor. Governments change, but nothing changes for us, or for their own deprived. Some of them would gladly swap their lives for yours. Huddled under bridges or in the corridors of the métro, the homeless must sometimes dream of a hut in Africa. Your political analysis makes me laugh. Your champions of hope are champagne socialists who turn the heads of the poor with hollow speeches and then go and happily stuff themselves with their good consciences. For all of us at the bottom of the heap, the left's still our mother, but she's a mother who all too often refuses us her milk, happy just to show off her beautiful breasts. As for their integration policy, it only applies to their national football team. *Blacks, Blancs, Beurs* – Blacks, Whites and Arabs – is nothing more than a slogan stuck on their international showcase, like a bad Benetton ad, it's just a recipe – *braised beef and butter* – which the TV channels fight over for millions. Foreigners are accepted, loved, are even in demand only if they're outstanding in their field. *Blacks, Blancs, Beurs* – if French society were truly integrated, they wouldn't need to invent a slogan. It's simply for show, to hide the grim facts from us.'

'And what are you offering in exchange for this dump? Eh?' cried Garouwalé, who was so carried away he'd forgotten to finish his tea. 'What are you offering? To feed us as long as your holiday lasts? And then what are we supposed to do? You suggest we just wait patiently here until we starve to death? Well, the answer's no! It would be better if you took your brother with you instead of making excuses to leave him here. You know everyone thinks you're selfish for not helping him leave. We'll manage without you; we're going whatever the cost. Our parents will grow old without a pension, our little brothers and sisters are depending on us! *Every scrap of life must serve to win dignity!*

'We have to face facts, kids,' advised Ndétare in a fatherly voice. 'Samba's leaving, but he's likely to come back with his suitcases full of disappointment. Marx's ideas are dying out here as well as over there, and the trees of hope we planted in 1968 have produced only very meagre fruits. Modernity's left us high and dry: apart from the pill, we haven't got anywhere. And, even the pill will have to be introduced in genetically modified rice, I reckon, to make women take it; their husbands are still in the dark ages. If only they'd stop measuring their virility by the number of children they produce. That too, boys, is underdevelopment, and it's part of a mindset. Try not to repeat your fathers' mistakes and you'll find you have more chances to get away than they did, even without going overseas. OK, be prepared to leave and head for a better life, but not with suitcases – with your brain cells! Rid your heads of some of the deeply ingrained habits that tie you to an outmoded way of life. Polygamy, too many children – all that helps sustain underdevelopment. You don't need a maths degree to grasp that the more people there are, the less bread there is for each person.'

As usual, Ndétare spoke passionately. His long twirling hands seemed to be drawing the opaque bubble where the meaning of his words eddied. The boys' attention was elsewhere, out of reach. They were oblivious to reason. I silently admired the schoolteacher's patience. How could I make these kids understand that it wasn't easy to live in France, when I myself had lived there so many years? No words will help, however well-intentioned. Sometimes it's easier to sit back and allow others to keep on to the end of the blind alley; sickened, they'll realise for themselves they've wasted their time and need to turn back. I walked out of the sitting room and left the angry boys to their brooding.

10

I NEED SOME AIR! WALK, FAST. I'm panting for breath. Outside, the coconut palms swayed, seeking an ideal position, and their manes seemed to push back the atmosphere's blue lid. Walk. Slowly. Breathe. Suddenly I felt alone. Who could I talk to? Childhood friendships may withstand time but never distance; our different paths divide us and leave us only a list of names that gradually come adrift from faces and their once-comforting melody. Back home, I missed being elsewhere, where being 'the other' is my fate in a different way. And I thought of those over there who find my sadness understandable and comfort me when I'm homesick for Africa. Several faces came into my mind. Freeze-frame! And here they all are, smiling at me; I'd have given anything to have them beside me. To talk about missing France on my native soil would be seen as betrayal. I had to carry this melancholy like an illegitimate child, silently and contritely. Always in exile, with roots everywhere, I'm at home where Africa and Europe put aside their pride and are content to join together: in my writing, which is rich with the fusion they've bequeathed me.

I was still pacing up and down to calm myself when Ndétare's friendly voice broke in, soft as consolation: 'Come, let's have a cup of tea at my place. I have some *bissap* in the fridge. That should make a little French girl suffering from the heat feel better, unless you prefer a coconut.'

'I like both, if "teacher" doesn't mind.'

We set off towards his place which adjoined the school. Seeing he'd brought back my smile, Ndétare went on: 'You know, you have to try to understand them. Most of these boys inherit nothing but mouths to feed. Many of them are already heads of large families despite their young age, and they're expected to succeed where their fathers failed: in lifting their family out of poverty. They're burdened with responsibilities that are too much for them and drive them to the most desperate solutions. I try to reason with them, but I know all too well that their anxiety about the future makes them belligerent. All those children to raise, with so little money...'

We continued talking as we walked. 'We should pay more attention to women's health,' he said, and I was delighted to hear these words from a man. Ndétare was the only man on the island who campaigned with the male nurse for family planning. As head of the primary school, he occupied a strategic position that enabled him to measure the comparatively high birth rate. As well as his packed classrooms, the geographic location of his accommodation gave him a prime observation post. He lived just behind Lake Nguidna. Reaching this spot, I paused.

'You used to play here, too, my dear,' he said, smiling.

'Can we sit down for a minute?' I asked, making myself comfortable.

He did likewise, in silence.

Nguidna, between the old village of Niodior and the new district built up on the Diongola dune, is a small lake, round as a chicken's arse and shallower than a witch's cauldron. A few narcissistic coconut trees and migrant palms from the Arabian desert, feign sentry postures so as to admire themselves at leisure in this lidless eye. This lake irrigated the memory of my childhood, causing reminiscence – that clambering plant – to germinate and sprout.

We listened to the evening breeze whispering in the foliage. *Kork! Kork!* The sun had just extinguished its smile and already a cane toad was trumpeting the start of the nocturnal concert with a deep croaking, which he and his fellow toads kept up non-stop. The chorus soon teased the tops of the coconut palms and the pious ears of the muezzin who, armed with his faith, bombarded the silence of the village.

'Well, it looks as though our tea has turned into supper,' said Ndétare. 'Shall we eat? If you want to rekindle your memories of playing on the mud shore, you'll have to come back in daylight.'

At the first rays of sunlight, the cane toads' chorus would die down. In the afternoons, huge black balls would emerge from the water, atop agile little legs, whose movement pierced Lake Nguidna's supple skin. Tadpoles? No, not exactly. A jubilant cheeping rose from the watery nest. The closer you got, the better you could see, on each of the balls, a double row of white pearls beneath two roving cowries. This phantasmagorical vision came into focus when you stood still on the shore and imitated the steadiness of the coconut palms that fringed the lake. Then you'd see shoals of children, boys and girls, filling their mouths and spouting water missiles at each other. They'd emerge, robed in innocence, run and roll in the warm sand for a moment, and then rush back in to cool off. Each time they dived in again, they'd stage a mock naval battle with empty coconut shells serving as torpedoes, only hitting their make-believe targets with the collusion of the enemy. Other imaginary regiments marched through the village alleyways, invading the squares, where they acted out the horrors of adult wars, seen on TV, as if to ward them off.

The number of children in the village is impressive. Nearly all the women of child-bearing age walk around with a baby on their back or under their clothes. Children arrive out of the blue, a shower of happiness or a worrying cloud of locusts, depending on how you look at it. Some families have enough kids to make up their own football team, subs included. And as for those who are polygamous, their hearts divided, they could even organise their own tournaments at home!

In the quiet of Ndétare's veranda, we shared supper, tea, the moonlight and all the thoughts that prompted the villagers' hostility towards us. What would become of these hordes of offspring? All those legions in third-world areas coloured red on the map, soon decimated by AIDS, dysentery, malaria and the economic bazookas aimed at us from the west. Devaluation! Demolition of our currency, of our future - of our lives, pure and simple! On the scales of globalisation, the head of a third-world child weighs less than a hamburger. And the women don't stop! Blind or blinded, they rush to sacrifice themselves on the altar of motherhood, to the glory of a god who gave them nothing but ovaries to justify their existence. At the well, in the fields, in the market-places, cannon fodder on the front line of poverty, they ask their bodies to keep giving until the very last breath of life. Ndétare told me about two of my former classmates who'd died in childbirth. Here, no one counts the number of women who die giving birth, or newborn babies who perish for want of medicines, but that doesn't put anyone off. Promptly buried, they're forgotten as quickly as dreams. Since our stelae afford no shade, let the wind flatten the island's sand! Fatalistic artisans, the mothers continuously make and replace countless little soldiers who they wish were made of lead to survive poverty's sharp teeth. Here, clinging to the gum of the earth, the poor no longer fear life's storms; they know the Atlantic only swallows them out of pity.

The embers of the stove were cooling, and the pagan dance of the coconut palms had slowed; the croaking of the cane toads was interuppted only by the clinking of the cups that the schoolteacher was rinsing. Sombre thoughts, we knew, were hardly suitable for a holiday evening atmosphere. Anxious to create a more relaxed mood, Ndétare produced the pearls from his collection of school howlers and began to tell the beads of our shared memories.

'Do you remember that hilarious day in class when I asked you – it was in the fourth year – what you wanted to do when you grew up?'

We burst out laughing. That day, quite a few boys answered primary-school teacher, nurse, policeman or sub-prefect – civil service professions we were familiar with in the village. Ndétare then asked them the reasons for their choice. Unanimous reply: because they had nice clothes, earned money and didn't have to go and work in the fields. Then a girl had put up her hand and announced: 'And I want to be a mummy!'

'But that's not a profession, is it?' Ndétare remarked with a wry laugh. 'You need a profession, a job, to earn money, to earn a living, do you see?'

'Yes, it is! It's even a good job! My father says that by being a mummy you can earn your way to paradise, and that's much better than money. To buy things, it's up to the man to decide, it's up to him to bring in the money. When I'm grown up, I'm just going to be a mummy, like my mummy, and I'll obey my husband so I can go to paradise, that's what my father says.'

'Oh yes, my dear!' teased Ndétare, disappointed, but laughing heartily. 'You're very likely to go to paradise, and maybe a lot sooner than you think...'

The teacher's explanations were drowned by giggling. The girl's brother raised his hand.

'Oh no! Not you! I suppose you're going to tell us you want to be a polygamist with a mission to increase the number of Muslims on the earth. I bet that'll open the gates of paradise, too, won't it?'

'Yes, sir,' the boy solemnly agreed. 'That's what my father says.'

It's hard to sustain forced laughter; although we wanted to keep things light-hearted, we couldn't find anything appropriate to talk about. It made more sense to go and confide the day's troubles to our pillows. The moon was drowning in Lake Nguidna. It was late in the night, the lights had gone out in all the windows except my grandmother's; Ndétare walked me home. At the door, he paused: 'You know, more than twenty years on, there are still children who are saying the same old thing. And it's even worse since the preachers have begun crossing the desert to spread their religious obscurantism around here. It's hard to believe that in our once animist, pagan land, you see more and more women wearing the veil now; some of my pupils come to class veiled, either copying their mothers or because they are forced to by a fanatical father fired with the zeal of the newly converted. Listening to the news, I realise that religious hypocrites are invading the country, opening institutes under cover of humanitarian aid and building Arab schools in remote parts of the countryside so they can spread their doctrine. But they're crafty, they keep out of sight; it's the people they control who do everything. Naturally, the state sees no harm in it and uses the excuse of progress to avoid resolving the problem. As with colonisation, by the time we wake up, it'll be too late, the damage will already be done. In exchange for a few benefits, communities with only scant knowledge of the Koran follow these obscure preachers like sheep. And anyway, why would our leaders want to attack those who come and do their job for them?'

The moon was wooing the clouds. I could picture the teacher's glum expression from the tone of his voice. But he was determined to leave me on a happier note: 'And you wanted to be Sokhna Dieng! Did you think I'd forgotten? Well, I haven't! Besides, I understand better now...'

Sokhna Dieng was one of the first women reporters for Senegalese television. As a child, I'd seen her on screen for the first time when I was staying in Kaolack with my grandmother. Back in the village, I'd often pick up newspapers, and then I'd run down the batteries of my grandmother's cassette player recording myself reading, trying my hardest to imitate Sokhna Dieng's voice and style.

'Stop it!' my grandmother would shout, exasperated. 'Only God knows when you'll be able to buy me batteries. That's enough now!'

'Please, just once more,' I begged. 'I want to speak French as well as Sokhna Dieng.'

Gentleness, grace, the apparent ease with which this woman spoke, her way of inviting her studio guests to speak with a supple hand gesture, without ever allowing herself to be interrupted, even by the most aggressive of them, fascinated me: a woman who had the right to speak!

The recollection made us explode with laughter. Even before Ndétare had time to draw his conclusions, I asked him: 'Is it better to be a child full of dreams and become an adult who can cope with disappointment or to be a child with no dreams and become an adult pleasantly surprised by the occasional success?'

Ndétare launched into philosophical analysis. The sitting room door opened, my grandmother poked her head in and feigned surprise: 'Hey, you two, your voices are shattering the night! What on earth can you have to say to each other that's keeping you up so late? Beware of this village; night is the preserve of witches, and at the hour when they're bringing out their cauldrons you're wandering around outside, easy prey, not waiting for the eye of day to guide you. *Athia, héye,* hurry up! You might have occult powers, but I don't. I'm going to shut the door.'

Make no mistake, these words were said with a stifled chuckle and boundless affection. They brought tears to my eyes. I thought of my solitary life in Europe, where nobody cared about my comings and goings, where only the lock on my door knew I was out. An e-mail or a message on the answering machine doesn't smile, doesn't worry, doesn't get impatient, doesn't empty a cup of coffee, still less a heart full of sorrow. While the total freedom and absolute autonomy we demand flatter our ego and prove our ability to be independent, they ultimately reveal a suffering as oppressive as the dependency we have escaped: solitude. When it's no longer in relation to others, freedom means nothing more than emptiness. The world is there to be grasped, but it embraces no one and doesn't let itself be embraced. The imaginary little chain that my grandmother stretched between us restored my equilibrium. After every storm, she is the beacon rising up from the belly of the Atlantic that sets my solitary navigation back on course. She has made me realise that there are no old people, only venerable beacons. Fixed, she's the ultimate anchor for my boatful of emotions launched onto the terrifying immensity of freedom. Her soft voice in the night was a mother's cool breath on the burns of her child. Ndétare knew this. He repeated his invitation for the next day and made a few polite remarks before disappearing, defying the spirits of the night. It had been a long time since anyone had waited up for him, and perhaps he secretly dreamed of falling into a witch's cauldron, so that at last something would happen in his life.

As I was no longer welcome at the boys' tea ritual, I went to Ndétare's house more often, and only my grandmother knew what time I came home. The Atlantic rumbled, the waves gnawed at the island's shores, no one said a word, but a warm, putrid breeze spread its murmurings through every kitchen yard. Since rumours are harvested faster than salt crystals, they were used to spice up the dinners. The atmosphere in the village became suffocating, and I slipped away.

11

I STILL HAD SOME MONEY LEFT, enough to afford a short stay in a small, unpretentious hotel. A trip to M'Bour, the town on the Petite Côte, south of Dakar, where I went to school for a time, turned out to be a good idea. First, the crossing to Djifère in a pirogue, then the express bus, which raised clouds of dust on the bumpy track to Joal where it joined a tarmac road. On arrival at M'Bour bus station I was assailed by a swarm of vendors. Taxi, quick!

That evening, I went for a long walk. Like an unfaithful wife, I needed to feel comfortable again in the places I'd left, at a time when I was still unaware of the wound concealed in the word homesickness.

In a bid to maintain its authority over M'Bour, the sea had sent its daughter Breeze to chase after Harmattan, the son of the Sahara, who'd stifled us all day long. The smell of the sea came in gusts. The moon was pale, but I met few people out walking. I soon realised why: in the distance, in the maze of streets, men who were still young competed with each other in a display of physical prowess. There was a wrestling contest going on for sure; the rhythm of the tom-tom alone was enough to confirm the nature of the event. The song that reached my ears clinched it, it was a wrestling song. No ambiguity as to the meaning: it was an appeal to male vanity, crooned by ebony sirens. I pricked up my ears, then began to whistle:

> *Lambe niila* (three times).
> *Domou mbeur djéngoul, beuré, dane.*
> *Do sène morôme.*

Which means:

> *Such is wrestling* (three times).
> *Wrestler's son, put on your belt, fight and put down*
>   *your opponent.*
> *You are the stronger.*

I stopped for a moment, as if to absorb the magic of their rhythmic chant. I felt a surge of emotion. No daughter of Africa can remain indifferent to the sound of the tom-tom, even after long years of absence. It seeps into you, like shea butter in a bowl of hot rice, and makes you quiver inside. The dance becomes a reflex. It's not something you learn; it's feeling, the expression of wellbeing, waking up to oneself, a manifestation of life, spontaneous energy. Ram-tam-rammety-tam!

M'Bour night, let me hear the throb of your heart and, for you, I'll transform my muscles into kora[1] strings! Your head spinning with this ancestral sound, your feet buried in the cold sand of seaside evenings, there's no better way to drink in the sap of Africa. It's like a communion handed down from the beginning of time. Our loincloths may have been replaced by trousers, our dialects corrupted, our masks stolen, and we may straighten our hair or bleach our skin, but no technical or chemical know-how will ever be able to extract from our soul the rhythmic vein that thrills to the first notes of the djembe. Reason and sensibility are not mutually exclusive. Regardless of the blows dealt us by history, this rhythm remains, and with it our Africanness, whatever preachers of any stripe may say. Oh! It was so good to be there! I am so happy, I said over and over.

I stood still, lost in thought, and hadn't reached the place where the wrestling was taking place. Swept away by the god of the tom-tom, I was all set to become his priestess when suddenly I was dragged from my contemplation by an abrupt silence. The tom-tom had stopped, announcing the end of the contest. The moon gloried in its appearance and continued its course. I hadn't been able to admire the wrestlers' dance, but I didn't feel deprived. Promising myself I'd go there the next day, I returned to my hotel.

As I was crossing the lobby, the receptionist, who appeared to be waiting for me, came to greet me, armed with a pathetic smile: 'Good evening, madam. My wife has just given birth. She's at the hospital, she's not well. She needs medicine which I can't afford. I know madam will understand. So I was wondering if you would be so good as to help me and save your sister? The baby's a girl. I'll call her after you; you have a pretty name.'

I burst out laughing, I found his shrinking look funny. 'Are you Muslim?'

'Oh yes! Like most Senegalese.'

'And this is your first child?'

'Yes, our very first!'

'And you want me to believe that you're going to name her after me? Save that sweet talk for the tourists.'

We both burst out laughing: my name, one of the most common first names in Senegal, is often given to the first-born daughter in Muslim families. What's more, it's so easy to pronounce that foreign-aid workers like to use it as a nickname for their maids. The receptionist laughed good-humouredly, realising I'd seen through his ploy. The hospital, medicine and tremulous voice were a con. He wasn't the only one to use such tricks to try to rip off the supposedly well-off over from France. I'd encountered a better actor than the receptionist on my island already: one fine morning a man came with tears in his eyes to ask me to pay for a prescription for his sick son, and persuaded me to dip into my pocket. That same afternoon I saw this bedridden son of his streak across the football pitch like an arrow and strike terror into the opposing team.

'In two days' time, just before I leave, I'll see if I have something left over for you.'

'OK, madam, that's kind of you,' he said, laughing.

He wished me good night, his cheeriness tinged with shame. When I'd arrived, in the early afternoon, he'd been reluctant at first to give me a room: 'Your ID card? Tell your client he has to pay for the room in advance,' he'd said.

'What client? How dare you?' I'd retorted before thinking better of it. 'I'm on holiday. Here's my passport and my French residency permit.'

'Ah, a *Francenabé*! My apologies, madam. Welcome to our country. Give me your bag and I'll show you to your room.'

After inspecting the place and finding everything more or less up to scratch, I'd sunk down on to the bed. The receptionist's words echoed in my mind. *Welcome to our country*, as if Senegal were no longer mine! What right had he to treat me like a foreigner, when I'd handed him an ID card just like his? A foreigner in France, I was treated like an outsider in my own country: as unacceptable with my residency permit as with my identity card. Strange as it may seem, it was thanks to my French residency permit, the guarantee of my creditworthiness, that I'd been able to get a hotel room in my own country. Then my anxieties about identity were driven out by the echo of his words: *Tell your client...* Before finding out I'd come from Europe, he'd assumed the purpose of my stay was disreputable. I didn't hold it against him: in general, third-world hotels are only for tourists' benefit.

The seaside resort of M'Bour is crawling with hotels. Most of its inhabitants have never seen beyond the façades. The only locals privileged enough to step through their portals are generally employed as receptionists, valets, chambermaids, cooks or drivers.

The hotels stand there, hideous on their gilt pedestals. As the state is so keen for revenue from tourism, it lets foreign investors take over the most beautiful stretches of coast and pay their staff peanuts. Steak for the powerful, the bone for the poor! So be it in the kingdom of capitalism which stretches into the shade of the coconut trees. Rats that eat less live longer, so we still have that glimmer of hope! But do anorexics still need a slimming diet?

Let the hotel industry operate for the pleasure of western tourists! Don't be too particular about what they do there, and whatever happens don't upset them. You want the customers to come back! Too bad if a few lecherous visitors come only to admire the landscapes of black buttocks instead of the Pink Lake, the island bird sanctuary, our empty grain stores and our picturesque shanty towns. Besides, to make ends meet, some receptionists will rustle up a few cinnamon beauties on request, high-class prostitutes with honeyed smiles, who are used to dancing the rigadoon. It makes a change from paperwork.

As for the girls who aren't pretty enough to hope for the receptionist's phone call or who optimistically trust to fate, they pace the hotel corridors tirelessly, from the shores of the Atlantic to the heart of Bamako, repeating the standard formula: *Love's passing.* But love always passes them by, leaving them out in the cold. Experts of many talents, willing to do anything, but unable to afford to inflate their breasts with silicone, they listen to their heels clacking down the long corridors, as they wait to expand their clientele thanks to the surgeon's scalpel. Tired of patching up the victims of tribal warfare for paltry salaries, African surgeons will have to reconcile themselves to amputating the political gangrene or cashing in on the high-class whores by mass-producing tropical Barbies.

So you gentlemen punters, when your well-gratified little dick is exhausted and deflates, begging for rest, be good enough to inflate the bill - that will please *mameselle*, even if your head would fit into her bra cup. If, on the other hand, you prefer non-genetically modified products, and you're tired of pneumatic tits, this native woman – so authentic, so natural – will be faithful to you and fulfil your needs, on each of your trips. But please gentlemen, spare her your smirk when she grabs your money muttering '*Merci, c'est riz*' instead of '*Merci, chéri*'; don't imagine it's a speech impediment. And if by chance she gets carried off by AIDS and stands you up, you can always go and whisper sweet nothings to her at the Bel-Air cemetery: that won't hurt your wallet.

For the female tourists who come to reawaken their hormone-deficient bodies, nothing could be easier: in exchange for a few notes, a chain or a watch not even made of gold, a stallion will press his six-pack against their sagging breasts and spray them with his nectar until the end of the holiday. After which, all those Africa-lovers will return home, tanned and tingling, showing off their photos of Sandaga market and a mask bought from a stall: 'Oh, Senegal's a wonderful country! We'll definitely go back!' And they keep their word. In the ocean, the shipwrecked can't tell the difference between the papaya tree and the ebony tree; they cling to a raft, that's all. Ladies and gentlemen, welcome to Senegal!

Young African women still wet behind the ears, their

sights aimed high and their bellies empty, marry decrepit westerners whose only charm lies in their wallets. They think they've happened on a diamond mine.

Behind the African beaches or in concrete European apartment blocks, there are countless African Venuses who go to bed every night like Jesus went to the Cross. Resigned, they look after their dinosaur and clean his false teeth, hoping for the pleasure of a trembling touch or the compassion of a passing plumber. Aware of carrying around a useless womb, they hope to be widowed before the menopause and battle to keep their looks. Poverty's martyrs, their only consolation is the money they send home to feed their families. Here, brothers, take and eat, this is my body, withered, western-style, for you! No hosanna! Just a requiem. The ebony Adonises in the same situation are more fortunate. Some find themselves a second wife, leaving her behind, but coming to visit her every so often to guarantee their lineage.

As well as bringing a flood of pathetic elderly tourists prepared to pay for a spouse, the tourist industry also attracts hordes of sickos with a penchant for fresh meat. The treasures that draw this type back again and again aren't listed in any catalogue. They're chrysalises that haven't been given time to unfold their wings, flowers crushed before blooming. The Atlantic may wash our beaches, but never the stain left by the tourist tide.

After a few days' break in M'Bour, I went back to the village to end my holiday, my head full of images and songs of wrestling, my body relaxed by the occasional healing wave. So it was with no ill-feeling that I joined the boys for their tea ritual. Having calmed down since the previous week's stormy argument, I wanted to avoid any clash before my departure. Ignoring any allusions to France, I harped on about my stay in M'Bour: 'It was great to see M'Bour again. The town's changed a lot since I was at school there, but I was so happy...'

'As happy as when you arrive in France?' broke in Garouwalé mischievously.

Still there, more impudent than ever.

Oh! Good old France, perhaps it's because she's always referred to in the feminine that men lust after her so ardently. The heckling didn't surprise me; it arose from the envy stirred by my imminent departure. I pretended to take no notice and, with an intention that was obvious to everyone, began telling the boys about the reception I'd been given on first setting foot in France, which, after all these years, was still fresh in my memory.

The plane landed at two p.m. and disgorged a multicoloured crowd that surged towards the arrivals hall. The professional smile of the stewardess standing on the gangway as we disembarked stretched over the *i* of Paris, as if to expand the city. 'Ladies and gentlemen, welcome to Pareee!'

A robotic voice, too sugary to have any taste, without an ounce of sincerity. Her face forgotten, the passengers formed two queues in front of passport control. At a glance, I identified which was moving faster and joined it, before spotting a notice: *EU passports*. 'Damn! I was almost there! And I thought apartheid was over,' I fumed, leaving the line.

In front of the other desk, where the uniformed officer couldn't even see the end of the queue, there was another sign: *Non-EU passports*. I took my place. Gradually the distance separating me from the eye of the nation diminished. I shuffled forward half a metre at a time, dragging my suitcase behind me. Suddenly voices rang in my ears. In front of me, two Africans were jabbering in a language I'd never heard before. Curious, I wondered what on earth this couple could be getting so worked up about, and above all what language they were speaking. Having strained to eavesdrop to no avail, I tried to quell my curiosity. After all, there are said to be at least eight hundred languages in Africa, according to George Fortune. Lucky there's French and English, otherwise the Organisation of African Unity would have to communicate by tom-tom.

An interminable wait, and it was the turn of the African couple to present their papers.

'Sir, one, your residency permit expired a week ago, and, two, this is not madam's passport. The woman in the photo is much older than her. You will not be allowed to remain on French soil!'

Gazing at the exasperated face of the custodian of the nation, the young woman launched into a tirade in her language, as did her companion. The officer repeated his words louder, but the African didn't seem to grasp what he was saying and continued his explanations, whose meaning evaporated with the misty spirals escaping from his mouth.

Teetering on my high heels, I shivered as I watched the scene. My skirt and low-cut top, ideal for the thirty-degree temperatures of Dakar, now showed their shortcomings faced with the three-degree weather in Paris. A coffee, God, a coffee, I'd have given anything for a hot drink! In Senegal I drank my coffee in the morning and was amazed to see whites in films drinking coffee at all hours of the day. I suddenly realised that it formed part of their condition. The African and his companion, who'd turned to me seeking a friendly face, were feeling theirs.

I looked for explanations. Immigrants had told me some of their scams: some, who lived in France with a wife and kids, had no qualms about taking a second wife when back home on a holiday and smuggling her into the country on their first wife's passport.

The man hopping up and down anxiously in front of me had perhaps been less fortunate than them. Or maybe he just lacked common sense? He looked old enough to be the father of the woman who was squirming nervously beside him. Perhaps he'd taken a second wife who was too young to look like the first and trick the beady-eyed officials?

The officer rose and glanced at me, barking: 'Are they thick or what? What about you? Yes, you, do you speak French?'

'Yes, sir.'

'Well, translate what I say to them. My colleague is coming to fetch them. They will be taken into custody until we find them a seat on a plane, then they'll be sent back home, pronto!'

'I don't speak their language, sir.'

'What! That's unbelievable! How do you speak where you come from: with your feet, perhaps?'

No, with tom-toms, arsehole, I thought, suppressing a smile. But I didn't breathe a word. I bet he'd never read George Fortune who, in any case, was probably making it up. He made a phone call. Two police officers appeared out of nowhere and greeted the couple, then showed them to their accommodation, a place that doesn't feature on postcards of Paris.

The officer settled back into his seat. I held out my papers.

'You know, sir, according to George Fortune...'

'I don't give a toss about your George or his fortune. What pisses me off is seeing you all, the whole lot of you, coming to seek your fortune here.'

He carefully read my proof of address and scrutinised my passport.

'You have a tourist visa for three months; your accommodation's only guaranteed for two months, so your stay is restricted to two months.'

'Yes, sir.'

'And?'

'Yes, sir.'

'What do you mean, yes? Your traveller's cheques and plane ticket, dimwit!'

'Yes, sir.'

'Stop bleating and get a move on. We haven't got all day, damn it!'

Everything was in order. The traveller's cheques amounted to the requisite one hundred French francs per day for the duration of my stay. The visa was in the right place in my passport but, as it was the first, the custodian of the state was suspicious. He'd had enough of African holidaymakers with a single visa and a one-way ticket; they always end up squatting   the churches of France, eating in the soup kitchens, buttering up the social workers, confessing to Abbé Pierre and demanding the right to vote. The sight of my return ticket reassured him. Whew! I could at last cross the barrier and step onto French soil. The thorns awaited me further on.

As I talked, I watched the boys' faces for signs of sympathy or despondency. I saw none. Garouwalé punctuated my story with a sarcastic comment: 'So you must love thorns? Otherwise you wouldn't keep going back there. I'd like your thorns, I would. The cow shits in the field where it grazes, but it only makes the grass grow stronger! Ha! Ha!'

Irritated by these fruitless exchanges, I stayed away and began to prepare for my return, coping as best I could with my end-of-holiday blues. I always had a tremendous sense of dread before going back to France, but I never told anyone.

Am I not, for them, the lucky creature who's flying off to France? Even in my own family, few were sensitive to my mood. The only ones I could trust to understand my sorrow and comfort me were my grandmother and Ndétare. My farewells to the boys were brief. And yet, on the day of my departure, everyone came to the landing stage to see me off. Africa's so warm! Besides, time, distance and homesickness eventually transform the bitterest anger into songs of love.

12

A FEW MONTHS AFTER MY RETURN to France, Madické and I were still at odds, even though, paradoxically, distance had brought us closer. The cost of phone calls no doubt made us avoid inflammatory subjects, even though the European Cup and its many extensions into extra time remained the symbol of our silent confrontation. All our conversations, even the most banal, turned into battles of strength.

'Hello!'

'Yes, it's me. Madické. Call me back.'

'Hi, how are you? What's wrong? Why are you calling me so early? It's barely eight o'clock. How are the grandparents? Is everything…?'

'Fine, everybody's fine. What about you, what are you doing today?'

'Nothing special. I was up all night writing. I'm going to sleep.'

'What? Have you forgotten? Today's the Final, France–Italy, six p.m. Senegal time; that's eight p.m. your time. Don't forget to watch the match.'

'OK. Let me get some sleep.'

'Please put your alarm on, I'm relying on you. You absolutely have to watch it. They tried to repair the Parisian's TV, but it's hopeless; it stops and starts when it feels like it. I don't know whether we'll be able to get the whole match here. So I'm counting on you. Shall we call each other after the game?'

'OK, but don't expect a blow-by-blow account. I'll just tell you the score. These phone calls cost a fortune!'

'Yes, OK, OK. Don't forget to set your alarm. Talk to you later.'

'Bye! Little tyrant!'

He'd hung up. I grumbled to myself: 'I don't need a goddamn alarm for your goddamn match! Honestly!'

Before going to bed, I set two alarms, one repeat alarm and one that imitated the sound of cowbells, bringing to mind the image of cows ambling around a meadow. Save the intervention of some evil spirit, I was certain to see Zidane make the Italians puke up their pasta and Maldini make the French choke on their *steak-frites*. An entire nation was about to laugh at the other's suffering. Two stud-booted armies were to replace governments in the confrontation. Madické was right: I mustn't miss this battle of shins.

As for the alarm, he'd kicked the ball right into the top corner, and I'd obeyed. But did he have any idea how much more he demanded of me? For some time now he'd been the ringmaster in the circus of my mind. His desperate wish to emigrate and the role he'd assigned me kept me awake at nights. Nights of questioning, nights of writing: brain meltdown. The juice? Words spun like cotton, woven, and plaited to form the invisible line that links the shore of dreams to that of life. Wound-words that burned my eyes, while he thought I didn't care about his fate. How could I get him to see that I wasn't refusing to help him? That, having discovered how hard the journey is, I couldn't agree to be his guide to the promised land? I don't have a magic wand to part the waters; I have only a pen that tries to forge a path that he can't take. However, in opposing his wishes, what could I offer him to prove that emigrating is not the only route to salvation? For the time being he was up against the reality of being a citizen of the third world, while I was following my Ariadne's thread in France.

I soon realised all my verbal barriers were useless. I was beginning to think that helping him come up with a scheme that was workable on the island was the best argument. But I still had to hit on the right idea, enticing enough to persuade him to put down his imaginary suitcases. Since the Atlantic doesn't make corn grow, my sweat had to fertilise the stretch of white sand where I was asking my brother to plant his dreams. And to do that, I had to save money. Like my cousin in the Sonacotra hostel, I'd quite simply given up on western luxuries. My leisure activities amounted to the number of dance steps I executed in my hallway, after long hours spent at the computer. The telephone was the umbilical cord that linked me to the rest of the world. Even shut away indoors, you continue your existential journey.

Now that he was faced with his own journey, Madické felt disorientated and expected me to set the pace in his uncertain race towards the future. I was stubbornly taking a route that didn't lead to France, where he was determined to touch down at all costs. A viable project on the island was all I could envisage. After leading a Malthusian existence for a certain time, I'd saved up some money, a small sum for France, but a fortune back home – enough to open a shop on the island. Nothing earth-shattering; just a grocer's. It would never be listed on the Stock Exchange, but it would provide a means of making a living that was more secure than fishing and less perilous than being an illegal immigrant. The morning of the European Cup Final, as Madické spoke to me on the phone, he had no idea of this nest egg set aside for him, nor of the plan taking shape in my mind. But after a sleepless night, I needed to muster my strength before launching into what promised to be a stormy argument. I'd gone to bed after his phone call, telling myself I'd unveil the plan to him another time, when his attention wasn't monopolised by the football news, which kept him on tenter-hooks.

At the hour when, with a quick glance, the baker counts how many croissants are left, when motorists converge on the city centre, when tides of still-drowsy pedestrians revive the streets, when grumpy executives sink into their padded leather chairs barking for their secretaries, at the hour when, at last, Strasbourg listens lasciviously for the murmur of the Rhine while offering herself up to the day's shy caresses, I was snuggling down under my duvet. It wasn't cold – it was summer – and yet, even though the doors were locked, I needed to burrow in order to shut myself off and begin my night in broad daylight. It was impossible to sleep. I flipped over like a pancake: as soon as one side of the bed became too hot, I rolled over to the other. Fed up, I kicked off the duvet, which now weighed a tonne. But it was no use. In front of my eyes, which bit into black, a screen began to dance. The prying eye of capitalism was pursuing me even into my bed, giving me orders: *Norton antivirus! Your Symantec subscription is about to expire! To continue receiving Live Updates, click on renew!*

Before going to bed, I'd done as instructed, believing the orders harmless. Nasty shock! The screen demanded 22.83 euros. 'Hold on a minute, honey. I didn't ask you for anything,' I'd muttered before clicking on *cancel*. And I railed against the moneygrubbers who've pushed their market boundaries right into our sitting rooms. Not content with having made us their captive customers, they manipulate us via the screen and levy their tolls from our purses via the Internet. 'No, this time I won't obey!' I shouted, stomping into my bedroom. But I was more enslaved to advanced technology than I thought. Slumped on my bed, I implored Morpheus in vain. My sleep was confiscated, one word blinking in the middle of my brain: Virus! Virus! Virus! I leaped up. No! My computer! I couldn't bear the idea of allowing it to be infected by electronic Ebola. Quick, a vaccine! I had to immunise it against all attacks, and too bad for my credit card – after all, it's only the painless blade that commerce has invented to slit our veins. I switched on again, my mouse conveyed my message of surrender, Symantec savoured its victory while giving me the illusion that I was acting freely: *Order confirmed!* 'Get lost!' I grumbled, going back to bed.

My head had barely touched the pillow when the echo of another dictator's voice started going round and round my mind: *Don't forget to watch the match...* I checked the two alarm clocks to be sure, but the voice was insistent. The day was advancing, my sleep retreating. I was supposed to be resting; I was wiped out. My upstairs neighbour started vacuuming, my temples were pounding, thump, thump, thump, and my nerves were tauter than the tom-tom of Doudou Ndiaye Rose, Dakar's master drummer. There was only one solution: wait for the start of the match in my bath. I poured in bubble bath – defying a doctor friend's many warnings – and inhaled the fragrance of synthetic coconut, relying on my melanin to withstand the evils of shower gel, when the doorbell rang. Dressing gown, quick! It was the postwoman with her lovely smile, bringing me a registered letter, the umpteenth summons from the regional immigration office about my application for naturalisation. I flung it onto a table and dived into the bath. There's just no way I'll ever get any peace, I thought.

On my arrival in France, before being issued with my residency permit, I'd been called to the International Immigration Office for a full X-ray. Free of scabies and pustules and not harbouring any shameful diseases, I'd been sent, along with a bill for 320 francs, a medical certificate, which stated: *Fulfils the requisite health conditions for authorisation to reside in France.* So illness is considered an unacceptable defect that bars access to French territory. Mind you, in the days when Negroes, ebony and spices were sold any which way, no one bought a sick slave. And in the colonies, for a long time the natives believed that the master never fell ill, so cleverly did everything conspire to maintain the myth of his superiority. The sick weren't allowed to go out and live in the colonies, and as soon as a colonist began to show signs of weakness he was quickly packed off home. Even today, the French army stationed in former colonies maintains special flights for repatriation of the sick, its ugly ducklings, and all those who disgrace the national flag.

Did the immigration office think it was teaching me to toe the line? One thing's for sure: they wanted to know everything about me. They'd seen me wearing Senghor's Negritude on my face and were unsure which role I could play in *Les Misérables.* They were determined to pursue their investigation, but this time my mind was made up: I'd reply to all their questions. I'd give them my vital statistics to prove that I take up less room than a certain pain-in-the-arse politician. I'd cook them a calf's head in peanut butter to prove I can perk up a President, restore his youth without cosmetic surgery and shield him from the barbs of his ambitious Prime Minister. I'd let them sniff my armpits, my favourite perfumes and deodorants. And lastly I'd let them count the number of holes in my knicker lace, measure the length of my hairs and, if they insisted, I'd disembowel myself to show them precisely where in my gut humiliation has set its leeches.

My bath had gone cold. I added more hot water, thinking of the young Africans who dreamed of being in my shoes, and made up a poem based on the traditional laments of my village. Up to my neck in foam, which slopped over the sides of the bathtub, I declaimed:

> *Shut in, cooped up,*
> *Captives of a land once blessed,*
> *Hunger our only comfort,*
>
> *Passports, permits, visas,*
> *And endless red tape,*
> *The new chains of slavery.*
>
> *Bank branch, account number,*
> *Address, ethnic origin,*
> *The fabric of modern apartheid.*
>
> *Perennial mother Africa suckles us.*
>
> *The west fuels our desires*
> *And is deaf to our hungry cries.*
>
> *African globalisation, generation*
> *Enticed, then sifted, dumped, ejected, wounded.*
> *We the unwitting travellers.*

That Sunday, 2 July 2000, my day had ground to a halt on the sofa when the alarm clocks let out their shrill cries; the European Cup Final would begin in a few minutes' time. A quick glance over the balcony told me that on this day of Our Lord Spherical Ball, there wasn't a soul in the streets. All the locals had retreated behind their four walls and were sitting in front of the media tabernacle. I made myself a pint of tea and switched on the TV. Before kickoff at eight p.m., the Italian and French national anthems rose up like prayers.

Which would reach the ears of God, no one could yet say. The camera lingered for a moment on the teams. For anyone who had trouble identifying the giants in each side, the already-hyper commentators gave a vivid rundown, plus a reminder of the teams' match history. It was the thirty-second match between France and Italy. Right from kickoff, Anders Frisk, the Swedish referee, realised that this would be no game of table football. France–Italy: with dozens of caps to his name, Didier Deschamps believed he had enough height to see the Italians coming, but Maldini was a head taller and intended to use the experience he'd gained in the international arena. For the entire first half, the two veterans eyed each other. Exposing then exploiting the opponent's weaknesses is perhaps not the most courageous of strategies, but it's certainly one of the most effective. Under the palaver tree, the wisest of the wise always speaks last. Respect! Barthez and Toldo grimly faced each other, and, unlike the fishermen, each of the two goalies was determined to bring home an empty net. Mounted on springs and programmed to block anything that was round, they were as alert as starving tigers, ready to pounce on even a soap bubble. No doubt, those two alone, manning the barricades in May '68, would have repelled the charges of the mounted police. The fans were going wild, yelling and chanting, trying to drown the noise from the other side.

Spanish bulls don't like red, and the Italians hate yellow, Frisk's favourite colour. In the first half, the Swedish ref dared to show his little card twice, to Di Biagio and Cannavaro, for excessive zeal. Delvecchio starts to see red and decides it's no more Mr nice guy. In the tenth minute of the second half, he sends a fireball to set Barthez's net alight. The French, their pride wounded, mount an attack on the opponents' goal – an eye for an eye, make them eat turf, the insult must be avenged. Careless of the respect due the two older players, Zidane fancies making a wig out of Maldini's long hair. He who walks towards God has no fear of crushing a king! Massive tension, shins burning, it takes a lot more than this to dent the two men's determination. Zidane's so tenacious he's awarded a free kick for France, but Toldo's there to curb his ambition and remind him of the respect he owes Maldini. Anchored to the ground, Lizarazu lets Pessoto dispossess him and run off with the ball. His nerves on edge, Thierry Henry lets rip and sends it flying over to Toldo, who's staunchly awaiting it.

Sensing danger, French manager Roger Lemerre follows the example of Dino Zoff, his Italian counterpart, and demands new blood. Fresh legs hit the turf, damp buttocks confide their fears to the substitutes' bench. Both teams dream of drinking champagne from the Cup, but first they must fill it with their sweat. There's no place for manners on a battlefield: Zidane's swapped his legendary cool for the fighter's ferocity, which prompts him to commit a foul on Albertini that's spotted by the ref. To think they compare him with Gandhi! In competition, pacifism in a great sportsman is like chastity in a streetwalker. They're coming up to full time. Anxiety and nerves are playing havoc with the French players' coordination, and even the best of them resort to blows below the belt. In the stands, the superstitious are crossing their fingers, wishing they hadn't put the champagne on ice. If the Italians are gasping like carp now, their saliva's beginning to have the sweet taste of victory.

It is then, two dribbles from the final whistle, that Sylvain Wiltord decides to ruin their appetite by scoring the equaliser that puts the counter back to zero and delays the feast. The Italians are reputed to have stamina in bed, but this evening the beauty they desire is playing hard to get and wants to be sure they're capable of equal tenacity on the pitch. *Mamma mia!* After a brief pause, with no kisses or even a peck, the two teams launch into extra time. Despite their efforts, the two camps have been unable to keep the match to a humanly bearable length. Stretching their muscles to the limit, the leather bubble has drawn them into this war of attrition. They know the king's sceptre will go to whoever lasts longer but not necessarily to the best. At this stage in a match, it's no longer about talent; only a goal offers salvation and earns the scorer the gratitude of an entire nation. With the energy of despair, every kick, even badly aimed, spirals towards the goals. No time to think, just keep teasing wilful lady luck, who'll do exactly as she pleases. Trézéguet's moment of glory comes quicker than he'd hoped. In the thirteenth minute of extra time, he scores the golden goal that plunges the Squadra Azzurra into the abyss of defeat.

Victory's joyous clamour rings out all over France. As Trézéguet staggers under his team-mates' acclaim and vigorous embraces, while waiting to hug the European Cup as he's never hugged his wife, Albertini finds it hard to fight back tears. The Italian players are no longer a team, but little islands of disappointment and misery. You always win together, but the dish of defeat is eaten alone. After relaying the outpourings of joy in various parts of France, the angels of live broadcasting turn their cameras on the emptiness and desolation of the Piazza del Popolo, abandoned by the bruised fans. The French reporters point out cruelly that in a hundred and eleven international games, Paolo Maldini has never won a single title with the Italian team.

I thought of Madické, who worshipped him all the same. Had the man from Barbès' TV been working? Had it conveyed Maldini's sorrow deep into the belly of the Atlantic? In other words, had my brother seen the match? I imagined him alone and in despair, surrounded by his jubilant friends, who go berserk every time France wins – another outbreak of post-colonial syndrome. From my sitting room I could hear the shouts of joy and the honking of horns that were turning Strasbourg into a giant stadium gone mad. The TV dissected the match highlights in slow motion; the commentaries were no longer cautious, but triumphant and authoritative. Now that all the important things have been said, I thought, I'll make myself another cup of tea to give me the strength to report back to Madické, in case he didn't see his defeated idol's look of despair at the same time as I did. As I made my way back from the kitchen carrying my teapot, the telephone rang.

'It's me,' said a quavering voice.

'Hang up. I'll call you back.'

'No, there's no point. The picture on the Parisian's TV wasn't very clear, but we saw the whole match. It's unbelievable what happened. But even so, Maldini was brilliant, he gave it his all...'

'Yes, but stop idolising Maldini. The guy's collapsing, not from exhaustion but from the weight of his millions, and anyway he doesn't even know you're alive.'

Then, thinking better of it: 'Don't be upset. It's only a game.'

'But it's the European Cup! The Italians deserved to win. The Squadra led the game right to the end; it's so unfair! And it really annoys me. My friends all laugh at me. And they've all chipped in for a party tonight.'

'Well, go and join them. Be a good sport. At least it'll make you feel better.'

'No! I don't feel like it. They annoy me the way they always criticise all the teams except France. And tonight they're being totally hypocritical. OK, I'll say goodbye. Ciao.'

'Wait, wait. Don't hang up – or, rather, hang up and I'll call you back. I've got something to tell you.'

I understood Madické's disappointment, but I found his sadness, the tears in his voice and his anger with his friends a bit over the top. On the other side of the globe, he was carrying the entire burden of the Italian defeat on his shoulders and was more wretched than the Neapolitans. Unable to find the right words to console him, this seemed the perfect moment to tell him about the plans I was nurturing and the money I'd saved up for him.

'For me? But that's a fortune!' he exclaimed, bursting out laughing. 'Do you know how much that's worth over here? Are you kidding?'

'No, no, it really is all for you, for what I've just told you about, unless you can think of something better.'

'But it's more than the cost of a plane ticket…'

'I don't want to hear any talk of a plane ticket! The shop or a similar project, on Niodior, otherwise I'll hold on to my money and it'll be too bad for you. Now, I'm going to hang up. Think about it and let me know when you've made up your mind…'

'If you think it's better to try to get by at home, why don't you come back? Come and prove yourself that your ideas can work. This place where you want to keep me, yes, this place, does it still mean anything to you? No, it doesn't. Madam no longer feels at home here. You want me to stay put but you…so why did you get out?'

'Think about it and give me your answer. I'm keeping the money for a few more weeks. After that, if you don't want it, I'll use it for something else. As for the real reasons why I left, it would take too long to explain over the phone. Just ask Grandma, she'll tell you. Bye.'

It's late at night. Strasbourg has lowered its eyelids to sleep or demurely to avoid watching the intimacy of lovers and the nocturnal sorrows of others. It's always at this time that my memory chooses to project films shot elsewhere, under different skies, stories buried deep down inside me like ancient mosaics in a city's subterranean tunnels. My pen, like an archaeologist's pickaxe, unearths the dead and discovers remains, tracing on my heart the contours of the land that witnessed my birth and my departure. From incidents I once barely even registered, I now compose the sustenance of exile and, above all, the weaver's yarn supposed to mend the ties broken by distance. Homesickness is my gaping wound, and I can't help but dip my pen in it. Absence makes me feel guilty, sadness drains me, solitude licks my cheeks with its long ice-cold tongue, which makes me the gift of its words – words too limited to convey the miseries of exile; words too fragile to break open the sarcophagus that absence has cast around me; words too narrow to serve as a bridge between here and elsewhere. Words, then, always used in place of absent words, definitively drowned at the font of the tears to which they lend their taste. And finally suitcase words whose contents are contraband, whose meaning, despite the detours, leads to a double self: the *me* from here and the *me* from over there. But who can multiply themselves like Christ's loaves without falling from the arms of their own people? And above all, is anyone there to pick up the fledgling that's fallen from its nest?

Grandma would probably explain to Madické why I prefer the anguish of wandering to the protection of the hearth gods. When I was a child, she and my grandfather were the only ones who could understand my silences, who followed my uncertain gaze and sat up late into the night to talk to me about how I felt. She understands better than anyone how exile has become my fate. Generously, she said nothing of her own suffering but made me a gift of her trust and packed my first suitcase, crammed with my thirteen years. Already, as a child, incapable of any ulterior motive and unaware of the attractions of emigrating, I'd understood that *leaving* would be the corollary to my existence. Having heard too often that my birthday reminded people of a disastrous day and symbolised the shame my presence constituted for my family, I always dreamed of making myself invisible. I can still see the shadow that descended like a net cast over those faces lined with anxious furrows the minute a visitor, dazed by such a number of relatives, would ask who my parents were. My body bore indelible marks, the price of the affront branded on cursed flesh. For, in traditional society, while respectably born children are brought up by the entire community and protected by the respect owed their parents, those who aren't baptised have the sole right to be thrashed by anyone who's in the mood. No reason is necessary, as the never-forgiven offence of their birth justifies all punishment.

To prove her love to me, even my wonderful grandmother was forever murmuring: 'I had to suffer the loss of honour, bringing up an illegitimate child in this village; prove me right, be polite, brave, intelligent, beyond reproach.' To make me all of these things, her great severity reflected the enormity of her sacrifice. She didn't beat me, she attacked me. In the village, her furious thrashings, which always ended in her biting me, are as legendary as her determination to protect me in the face of all opposition.

I grew up with a feeling of guilt, an awareness that I had to atone for a sin that is my life itself. I lowered my eyelids as if trying to conceal my entire being. For a long time my smile meant: 'I'm sorry.' I expected my submission to earn me love, but in vain, so then I demanded respect. A rebellious teenager, I decided to do only as I pleased, always with the support of my grandmother, a feminist in her way. Wanting to breathe without offending anyone, so the beating of my heart wouldn't be considered sacrilegious, I stepped onto my boat and turned my suitcases into vanishing cases. Exile is my geographical suicide. Stripped of my history, I am drawn to foreign lands because they don't judge me according to errors of fate, but for what I've chosen to be; they are the gauge of my freedom, of self-determination. Leaving means having the courage necessary to go and give birth to oneself; being born of oneself is the most legitimate of births. Too bad for the painful separations and the kilometres of sorrow. Writing smiles at me knowingly for, free, I write to say and do everything that my mother didn't dare say and do. Identity papers? All the folds of the earth. Date and place of birth? Here and now. Identity papers! My memory is my identity.

An outsider everywhere, I carry an invisible theatre inside me, teeming with ghosts. Only memory offers me its stage. In the depths of my exiled nights, I beseech Morpheus, but recollection illuminates me and I see myself surrounded by my family. To leave is to carry inside you not only all those you've loved, but also those you've loathed. To leave is to become a walking tomb filled with shadows, where the living and the dead have absence in common. To leave is to die of absence. You return, of course, but you return a different person. On going back, you seek but never find those you left behind. Tears in your eyes, you resign yourself to noticing that the masks you'd made for them no longer fit. Who are these people I call my brother, my sister etc? Who am I to them? The intruder who carries inside her the woman they're waiting for, whom they despair of ever finding again? The stranger who turns up? The sister who leaves? My dance between the two continents is fraught with these questions. Madické has only added to them. A few months after our conversation, tired of waiting for his reply to my proposal, I sent him the nest egg. Then I waited, longing for news, but he seemed in no hurry to make contact.

13

IN NIODIOR THE SEASONS HAD no reason not to go on. Some brought an abundance of millet and fish, others not enough, but they all promised better times for humans, be they hopeless dreamers or fatalists, forgiving life its betrayals, the way a man head-over-heels in love is happy to ignore his sweetheart's little infidelities. Back there, nothing changed. The islanders still clung to the gum of the Atlantic which belched, extended its greedy tongue and withered the flowers with its hot breath. Always punctual for its appointment with the coconut palms standing sentry, the scorching sun asked only to show its own weariness. But on this June day in 2002, no one would pay it any attention.

As usual, the women had risen at cockcrow to lower their buckets into the wells, refill the huge earthenware jars for the family's showers, chop wood and clatter about in still dark kitchens, before coaxing the fire to cook the breakfast of millet porridge whose smell would soon fill their homes. The dunes to the east were tinged with orange. The miserly sky quietly gathered its gold. For the time being, the palaver tree only harboured the cheeping of birds, and only the smoke from the kitchens lingered in the alleyways. Few pirogues had left the island's landing stage. And yet, it wasn't Friday, but Sunday, the day of a God who has no stray sheep in these salt pastures.

In a sitting room, a gleaming television set sat imposingly on a fine teak table. There was no space left on the matting spread before it. A young man was pacing up and down, holding a remote control. A young woman entered carrying a huge bowl of millet porridge which she carefully put down on another table. She disappeared through the door, then came back with a stack of bowls and a little plastic tub overflowing with vanilla-flavoured sweetened curds. The young man with the remote control brought spoons and handed them round to his guests, who immediately helped themselves. They ate without taking their eyes off the screen. Sitting in opposite corners of the room, Ndétare, on a chair, and the old fisherman, cross-legged on a mat, tried to conceal their mutual hatred, but the arrows darting from their eyes betrayed them. Only an exceptional circumstance could oblige them to meet under the same roof. To give an impression of composure, the old fisherman started telling the youngsters in a self-conscious voice how, the day before, schools of dolphins, each more graceful than the last, had swum alongside his boat right back to the shores of the island. His tale was met with relative indifference, so he tried to liven it up: at first it was fun, but then things became worrying; he'd never seen such a rough sea! The dolphins cut across the path of his pirogue, and their unpredictable diving threatened to capsize it. Sceptical, his audience carried on eating breakfast in silence: dolphins aren't known to be aggressive, quite the opposite. He wasn't going to persuade them that Nessie was lurking at the gates of Niodior. The latest arrival left his slippers at the door of the sitting room, adjusted his flowing gold-embroidered *boubou*, greeted everybody at length except Ndétare and came and sat down next to the old fisherman. The old sea wolf felt a little more comfortable: the newcomer, the man from Barbès, shared his enmity towards the schoolteacher. They exchanged a few platitudes about the start of the rainy season, and then the young man with the remote control drew everyone's attention to the reason for their gathering.

'I'm turning up the volume. It's about to begin; they're starting the national anthems.'

All eyes converged on the television. The Oita stadium was revealed, as imposing as a gladiatorial arena, the green turf lending a note of softness to the volcanic Japanese landscape. This corner of the earth was the land of the rising sun, so the commentators kept saying. But those assembled didn't care – the sun also rises behind the dunes of Niodior – they simply wanted to see the flames of victory shoot from the heels of their favourite players. Forecasts were flying on all sides; less stormy than usual, they rang out like Communion prayers. For once, the division on the pitch didn't extend to the group of young islanders. Astonishingly united, these fans had stayed up all night so as to be certain not to miss the start of the match, and now they were sticking together in the face of the anguish to come.

Since their first footballs made of old rags, their clumsy attempts at dribbling on patches of waste ground and their goals swollen with the pride of passionate adolescence, to their latest incarnation as boastful young adults, even in their wildest dreams they'd never imagined a line-up like the one that brought them together that morning: 16 June, Senegal v. Sweden in the second round of the Korea–Japan World Cup 2002! Even the island's most revered sorcerer hadn't divined it from the murmurings of the spirits he often invoked for his young believers' matches. He'd predicted Senegal's win over Cameroon, in Mali, in the African Nations' Cup 2002. But in the savannah the Cameroonian Lions were indomitable, and the Senegalese team, the courteous Lions of Teranga, went hungry. The sorcerer admonished his young customers for neglecting the required ritual; worse, they hadn't buried the grigri in the right place. The contrite youngsters nursed wounds which healed the minute it was announced that Senegal had qualified for the 2002 World Cup. Then they'd sung and danced. Oh no! Even if they were thrilled, they didn't go so far as to hope to celebrate with palm tree wine in this tournament. For once, Ndétare hadn't needed to lecture them. They were big on stoicism in the Olympic spirit: the fact that their national team was taking part was more important than the outcome. While braggarts caught up in Zidanemania considered Senegal a piece of cake, the young Niodior footballers slipped their pride under their grandmothers' pillows and let the Atlantic rumble its anger. Forgotten somewhere in the ocean, they caught only a weak echo of the excitement that had preceded the departure of the Lions of Teranga for Asia. Up until this morning when they sat with bated breath, the TV had become magical, their fount of happiness. The national team had won match after match, as if each time extending them a further period of grace; they never wearied of savouring their own commentaries on every match, like favourite sweets passed round at tea-time.

But for the moment Oita sounded like an exclamation; a new match was being played and no one knew what the outcome would be. While nerves gnawed at the young spectators, the old fisherman fingered his beads. Hunched on his chair, Ndétare had jumped several times before cupping his chin in his hands again. Suddenly, he leaped up, unfolded his giant form and doubled over as if he'd been kicked in the stomach. He, Mr Reasonable, Mr Placid, Mr Rational, let out a terrible howl of despair; the roar of a wounded lion filled the house. The Swedes had just buried the ball in the corner of the Senegalese net, despite Tony Sylva's vigilance. Clutching his beads, the old fisherman let out a volley of curses; it was an age since his son had been in the national team, but he was still passionate about the game. Calm was restored, resignation began to set in; for a while they all thought the dream ended here. But no traditional army ever won a battle without a measure of recklessness; a mixture of pride and blind optimism keeps the troops' faith intact. When defeat looms, shouting 'we're going to win!' is the last plea, and, in the sitting room, it fell to the irrepressible Garouwalé to pronounce it.

'Oh! Don't let yourselves get beaten, it's not over yet. We've come this far, we can still do it. I swear, they can't defeat us. We're going to win! I'm telling you, we're going to win.'

The crowd perked up a bit. Garouwalé had no grounds for his conviction, but he was full of hope, like his friends, after the recent victories over Denmark and Uruguay. Especially since that red-letter Friday, that historic date of 31 May 2002, he was fearless. With no publicity or propaganda, the humble Lions of Teranga had toppled the kings of the world. Defying all predictions, they'd sent the French team home faster than they'd ever thought possible, to taste the bitter bread of defeat. That day, in Asia, far from African masks and sorcerers, Goliath had been deprived of David's God. Since then, the youngsters on the island had new posters pinned to their bedroom walls.

Confidence had returned to the sitting room. The old fisherman's beads slid through his hand, but the tension remained palpable. Suddenly there was thunderous applause mixed with shouting: Henri Camara had just scored, allowing Senegal to equalise. Relieved, the young man with the remote raised the folded fabric lying beside him: the national flag. He patted it, smoothed it a little, then put it down again and ordered the young girl sitting next to him to serve drinks.

'I told you!' yelled Garouwalé. 'Lions eat meat, not grass. After the French cockerel, then Denmark and Uruguay, it's the Swedes' turn, and we still haven't had enough! We'll have them. It's only a matter of minutes, I'm telling you!'

But, like the old man's beads, the minutes went by one by one and the Lions chased that goal in vain. Every face grew anxious again. Jaws clenched, eyes creased, the youngsters greeted the whistle signalling the end of full time like a cold shower. Extra time was inevitable, and the short break felt like an eternity. The ads cast their nets in vain: minds were elsewhere. Outside, the sun gradually obliterated the shadow of the dunes, gangs of children made the most of their day of freedom racing around the village or stealing a few coconuts. Women swept the streets around their homes, while those on kitchen duty rummaged in the grain stores, kept a lookout for the occasional fisherman or took advantage of low tide to scrape the bottom of the sound in search of something to cook up for lunch. To pass the time, the old fisherman started telling the man from Barbès his dolphin story. Halfway through, the Oita stadium reappeared; he stopped talking and began pulling nervously on his beads again. The youngsters had left their original positions and were crowded in front of the screen. They didn't know the Sénefs – as the Senegal team was dubbed – very well, and the recent wins put the choices of Bruno Metsu, the coach, beyond criticism. Speculation gave way to silence, and even Garouwalé was at a loss for words to reassure the group. Then a wind of panic blew; they clutched each other as a tremor ran through them all. '*Allah Akbar!*' said the old fisherman, crushing his beads into his face with both hands. And God was good enough to send a breath of fresh air from Oita all the way to the Niodior sitting room. When the old man opened his eyes again, the youngsters were already breathing more freely. Tony Sylva hadn't intercepted the ball, but our animist ancestors were probably in Oita giving objects the power to come to his aid: the bar had stopped the Swede Svensson's shot. *Alhamdoulilah!* The threat was averted, but extra time was beginning to drag and it felt as if the clocks were standing still. Perhaps one of the worry beads had fallen into God's ear, because in a flash joy lit up every face.

'The golden goal!' screamed Garouwalé in the midst of the uproar, imitating the commentator. 'Henri Camara! He's scored again! It's the golden goal! Senegal's beaten Sweden! It's their ticket to Osaka! The Lions of Teranga are through to the quarterfinals of the World Cup! It's unbelievable!'

General uproar in the sitting room: arms flailing, everyone hugged the nearest person. Ndétare and the old fisherman found themselves embracing. When they realised, they exchanged embarrassed smiles. The man from Barbès, surprised by the sight, pretended not to have noticed and went on celebrating with the kids. Then the Oita stadium vanished from the screen and the ads came on. The young man with the remote, without even switching off the set, unfurled his flag and ran off towards the main street of the village. With his friends at his heels, he chanted victory, evoking the legend of the lion, king of the forest: 'Long live the Lions! *Gaïndé N'diaye! M'barawathie!*'

Two of the boys turned down a side alley and rejoined the group carrying djembe drums. They made up a dance in the middle of Dingaré, the village square, borrowing a famous tune by Yandé Codou Sène. Glorifying the lion, our national emblem, the song declares *the lion doesn't like greens, let him eat meat* - it couldn't have been more apt. Singing their heads off, the young people made up their own version. In their eyes, not only were the players in the national team lions, but, as well as eating meat, they said, they fed on goals, balls, dribbles and triumphant passing shots:

Khamguèné Gaïndé,
Gaïndé bougoule mboum, yâpe laye doundé
Gaïndé, Gaïndé,
Gaïndé bougoule mboum, yâpe laye doundé
Henri Camara gaïndé la,
Henri bougoule mboum, buts laye doundé
El Hadji Diouf gaïndé la,
El Hadji bougoule mboum, dribbles laye doundé
Tony Sylva gaïndé la,
Tony bougoule mboum, balles laye doundé
Bruno Metsu gaïndé la,
Bruno bougoule mboum, entraînements laye doundé
Les Lions de la Téranga
Kène bougouci mboum, victoires lagnouye doundé...

14

IN STRASBOURG THE CATHEDRAL contemplated the clouds' slow passage, while waiting to greet poet angels. The Rhine snaked its way, slapping the sides of locks, fleeing the boatmen who demanded back their wasted hours. It was summer; life was a vanilla-and-chocolate ice cream, a floating island in plunging taffeta, a kite string that excited kids and at nightfall, behind closed doors, slipped between adults' fingers or dragged them inexorably into autumn. As the storks exchanged their feathers for tattered dreams, I followed the World Cup, watching the matches on TV, leafing through the newspapers.

Not a single call from Madické, either to find out how I was or to ask for a match report. I pictured the celebrations back home. I watched a documentary showing the mother of El Hadji Diouf, the Senegalese striker, dancing for joy in her huge villa after a win. I said to myself: 'All the children of Senegal who eat sardines while they wait for God to spare them a thought would be thrilled to invite their mothers to join that dance. And for one single step of that dance, they're prepared to cross the Sahel on foot, die in the hold of a plane or on a raft launched on the slaughter-water from the Strait of Gibraltar. People die alone on the way, but they often set off for the sake of others.'

Moussa, who'd been unable to cope with the shame of repatriation, is no longer here to see his father finally realise that in our day and age football is a first-choice source of income; actually, it's the ideal emergency exit for third-world children. Better than the terrestrial globe, this round ball enables our underdeveloped countries to catch the west's fleeting gaze, which usually dwells on the wars, famines and ravages of AIDS in Africa. Yet to combat these, the west wouldn't consider donating the equivalent of the budget for a championship. So, naturally, with Senegal's World Cup triumph, the black population of France was singing and dancing; for once, they were invited to play with the big boys, who, what's more, were saying good things about them. Even those who were afraid to go home with their suitcases stuffed with failure, humiliation and disappointment came out of their cramped tower blocks to shout about their pride regained in France. They even managed to forget that no one ever spoke of gratitude towards them or even simply citizenship, but only of tolerance and integration into the mould of a sieve-society in which they are the lumps. But as the Parisian Senegalese rejoiced, parading down the Champs-Elysées, they were overtaken by their condition of immigrants and its corollary, contempt. The Arc de Triomphe isn't for negroes! Move along there, please! But in 1998, in Dakar, the French expats had blocked all the main streets and then taken over all the best restaurants. Drinking to the Cup into the small hours, they'd disrupted the city people's sleep with their endless honking of horns, and no one had criticised their drunken excesses. Exempt from visa requirements, they consider themselves at home, according to *teranga* – local hospitality – and the laws that the French impose on our leaders while still holding out on them. They have enough money to buy half the country and, as a bonus, commandeer imported vintages to celebrate their win until their thirst is quenched, unlike these immigrants, who get drunk on *bissap* juice so as to forget their miserable pay slip, if they've ever had one. Come on, move along there, please! Bunch of morons! Go dance the bamboula under your banana trees. You think this is Sandaga or what? I told you to move along, before I send you to la Gueule-Tapée.

And on they'd moved, unable to parade around the Arc de Triomphe: the boys in blue with their batons win every time, especially when the giant photo of Zidane, transformed into an urban tapestry, is no longer there to mesmerise them. Cries of jubilation in Wolof – now that wakes them up. It brings them out in spots. It annoys them so much they conveniently remember that their job is to ensure that motor vehicles are able to move freely down the Champs Elysées, and everywhere else on French territory, even on days of public celebration. It was all very well for the préfecture to try to wriggle out of the public relations fiasco by arguing that they had a duty to protect pedestrians, before admitting that people never ask for authorisation to express their joy, but the men on the ground weren't content to blush in the face of Wolof exuberance. OK, let's be fair; they have their jobs to do, that's why we give them batons. But sssh! Madické doesn't know any of this. Even if Africa is, as they say, full of tyrants, he'd only ever seen up close the island's two policemen who play football with him. So if ever you tell him I'm afraid of the cops, because of their brutal ID checks and their accusing looks, I sentence you to four hours alone with a patrol. I'm used to it, and I don't care; but you might not be.

It wasn't only the police who found the Senegalese immigrants' joy unpalatable. Some journalists claimed it was undeserved. Hijacking the Senegalese victories, they could hear the cock's crow in the lion's roar. It's true that most of the Lions of Teranga play in France – and Senegal can only be grateful to those who've allowed them to hone their talents – but is that good enough reason to consider them Senegauls, second-class 'blues', and deprive their country of the honours won under its flag? Have we ever seen a teacher award himself his pupil's diploma? Besides, if Socrates discovered minds, it's because they weren't empty in the first place. El Hadji Diouf wasn't born from Zidane's thigh. Football shirts, yes; leashes, no! Despite Schoelcher's efforts, the old master still buys Africa's colts, feeds them on hay and is proud of their performances. Since Africa is considered inept to the point of not even deserving its own sweat, its independence is a trap, and we should beware of the predator's claws. So I declare 2002 international year of the battle against colonisation in sport and the trade in footballers!

No news from Madické; the World Cup went on, and, with it, the takeover bid for Senegal. While the Senegalese made do with large mouthfuls of *thiéboudjène* and celebrated their successive wins with a little *bissap* juice, the cockerel was still dragging its wounded leg, and the parrots that tried to console it were still hitting a false note.

On 18 June all eyes were still turned towards Asia and the newspapers trumpeted: South Korea–Italy. Many were selling the Koreans' hide before the match had even started. I had little interest in the forecasts, but one thought excited me: I was almost certain that by the time Maldini's football shirt was all soaked in sweat, my brother would call me, to share his delight or his woes, who cared – I just wanted to hear his voice. So I watched the match, more to pick up on the details so I'd know what he meant when he wanted to discuss the finer points. I didn't want to admit it, but, deep down, I was praying for the Italians to win. It would make Madické so happy. Meanwhile, crammed by the thousand into the red stands, the Korean supporters exuded enough energy to propel their players to victory. After a long struggle, the moment of truth had arrived for the Squadra Azzurra. Proud and upstanding, when no one was expecting it, the Koreans subjected the Italians to the same fate the Senegalese had meted out to the Swedes. Despite the number of the holy trinity on his football shirt, Paolo Maldini, my brother's hero, hadn't been able to prevent the golden goal scored by the Korean player, Ahn Jung Hwan, who was determined to redeem himself after missing a penalty. Madické's giant didn't have feet of clay, but he'd missed the irreverent ball by a few centimetres and it flew over his head. Of course, I wasn't planning to describe it to my brother that way. Over the phone, I'd have said: 'Oh, Maldini really did everything right. He was just unlucky.'

The days went by and still nothing from Madické. I amassed a pile of football magazines to send him, all the ones that had articles about the Lions of Teranga, naturally, but also, as before, any paper that had a photo of Maldini or mentioned the Squadra Azzurra. But would my brother persist in worshipping this team if he knew how graceless some Italian football managers were and how they trampled the spirit of the game? Luciano Gaucci, president of the Perugia team, didn't wait for the end of the World Cup to announce that Ahn Jung Hwan, responsible for the golden goal that had knocked out Italy, had been dropped. Are African and Asian players, the seasonal workers of the football world, supposed to give up defending the colours of their native country in exchange for a fistful of euros? If the west can't handle being matched by the third world even in football, how can we hope it will help us attain a similar level of development? While the little countries were celebrating their unexpected entry into the big league and discovering its splendours, the headlines of a leading Italian newspaper screamed: 'A DIRTY WORLD CUP!' Would a clean World Cup be one played, refereed and won by our invincible European masters? Don't kick the ball into touch!

No phone call. I comforted myself as best I could: on his island, my brother had no master, he was going about his business freely, unaware of my questions. Perhaps he'd call me at the end of the championship. Then, fully informed, we'd be able to analyse the Senegalese and Italian performances. I had to keep abreast of events.

The tenacious Turks had blunted the lion's claws; Senegal had lost the quarter-final and was knocked out of the tournament. The dream stopped there. The World Cup went on, but my excitement gradually dwindled and my patience was wearing thin. Hostage to the media during this period when sport, without appearing to, established consensual totalitarianism planet-wide, I felt as if every second spent in front of the computer was an act of resistance.

Still no call from Madické. The exile is always missing someone, of course. But there are times when this deprivation turns bitter and transforms the other place into an open-air prison. Homesickness is a wound that can't be healed by a warm welcome. One person can't replace another. Friends' affection comforts, but it can never fill the holes that absence bores into the heart. Even a row with my brother over the phone would have made me feel better. So why didn't I call him? No, even if the wait was painful, I wanted to know if he was missing me. People back home aren't in the habit of phoning or writing to their relatives abroad except when they need something, or to inform them of a death. So, since there's always a motive for getting in touch, the person living abroad no longer knows where to look for signs of their family's feelings, of their affection. Do they ever think of us in a selfless way, purely from love? I was waiting for an answer to this question. I had to hold on a bit longer. Thinking non-stop, tormenting my brain, keeping my mind alert, my will active, refusing to allow it to buckle, and burying my doubts – that's what I had to do to keep despondency at bay. The Wailing Wall isn't in Strasbourg; we have the Rhine that keeps flowing, and flowing for ever, yet it doesn't give tears the taste of the Atlantic. Sweet and soft my Rhenish nights should have been if my brain weren't rocked by its perpetual swell. But what then was it murmuring, the ocean that reflected the shadows of my nights?

Over there, too, it had been announced that twenty-one of the twenty-three players selected for the national team play in France. On top of all the reasons the island's youngsters come up with to justify their wish to emigrate, wasn't this likely to be the crowning argument? Now that the whole world knew that our sportsmen, who are restoring our nation's pride, live in France, how could we dissuade our young people from thinking that they, too, should go and seek success there? Today, it's more important than ever for immigrants to speak out frankly, even those with the halo of success. It's not a question of putting our people off the west, but of showing them the other side of the coin. And I started fantasising about lectures during which every one of our Senegalese players would talk openly about the harsher side of their lives in France. I'd have them describe to their brothers the cold ashes of the fireplace whence the flame of victory leaps, piercing the shadows of exile. I'd have them talk about how, in Guingamp, Lens, Lorient, Monaco, Montpellier, Sedan and Sochaux – where they play – the same people who applaud them when they score a goal make monkey noises, throw bananas at them and call them dirty niggers when they miss a shot or falter in front of goal.

Let our valiant players tell their fans back home, who dream of joining them at European clubs, how some of them spend most of their time stuck on the bench, when they're not being used as stopgaps, or playing out of position to allow the established players to shine. 'You only ride a donkey if you don't have a horse,' says the farmer.

Pass the mike round! Let our heroes tell their brothers how much red tape they have to deal with: France takes credit for their feats on the pitch but very often grants them only a temporary residency permit. Just as we regularly have to update our subscription to Symantec's antivirus software, some players have to go and renew their anti-expulsion visa. Each year, a proportion of what their goals earn them ends up in the embassy's coffers, just so they have the right to breathe in the country of human rights. The price the Senegalese pay for a visa to come to France is the equivalent of one month's salary locally, whereas any French citizen can go to Senegal when he pleases, with no formalities. If you don't love or trust me enough to let me come to your place when I want, you'll have to learn to knock on the door when you want to come to mine. Are our players capable of such honesty?

Still no news from Madické. And yet he knew that, unless there was an emergency, I never took the initiative to phone him because it involved making two calls: the first to Ndogou, the call office receptionist, asking her to go and find him, and the second in the hope that he'd be on the other end of the line. Was he angry with me? Was he thinking that if I'd helped him to come and play in France, he might now have been one of those players they hero-worshipped back home?

The World Cup was over, the world order hadn't changed. The big advantage of the European Union isn't the non-stop shopping made possible by the euro or the enlargement of the territory for tracking down foreigners; it's the possibility of fighting on several fronts: after a national defeat, you can always pray that another EU country will win. In the World Cup Final, Germany was snowed under with flags. But the men whose names nearly all ended in an 'o' as round as the ball were determined to avenge their 1998 disappointment. Brazil won the Cup, and all the surprises of the tournament were forgotten. A great footballing nation had won as predicted; history, which had nearly veered off-course, was back on track. There were no more distractions; once again we had to face humdrum reality and carry on smiling at life through gritted teeth.

Abroad, depression always threatens to descend, for lack of anything occurring to restore taste and colour to the monotonous procession of days. For me, it took the unexpected form of a little parcel with six stamps from Senegal. Tearing off the wrapping paper, I found a box Sellotaped on all sides that had once held four radio batteries. It contained a little hand-sewn cotton bag inside which were squeezed three plastic bags, each containing a local product: a few groundnuts, some peanut butter and a handful of dried millet flour. This meagre parcel, which would make most people laugh, filled me with delight. This parcel meant that *over there*, at the ends of the earth, in the Sahel where the sand burns your soles, where the vultures are alone in celebrating the passing of the flocks, *over there*, in the belly of the Atlantic, where only salt is harvested in abundance, *over there*, where it would be wiser to hold on to one's paltry goods than give them away, someone was thinking of me with love. While Madické, who'd made a football reporter of me, remained silent, the boundless affection contained in this unexpected parcel filled the screen of my life. No one has taught the men back home that showing affection doesn't make you less of a man, that on the contrary it gives more soul to the strongest characters. If people gather under the baobab tree, it's not just because of its ability to withstand tempests, but also because it's capable of imparting and spreading the sweetness of its shade. It's not surprising that in Africa the children always play close to the women. While the tough guys treat them like plants, mothers and sisters graciously spread their shade, care for these fragile shoots who, from the age of seven, will refuse their kisses, turning into real dry-season baobabs. Madické had become what he wanted, a man, and he's not keen on whining girls, or moaning guys either, he used to tell me. I knew that the tone of my voice over the phone would only make matters worse – unless, for once, he'd consent to a conversation between equals.

That evening, as I was drinking my tea, quietly nibbling my groundnuts with delight, the telephone rang. Oh no! Not now! The ringing was insistent. I picked up the receiver.

'Yes, it's me, Madické.'

'Well, well, at last you're good enough to call me! Hello, sibling! So tell me, who do you want to talk to? Your ticket for France or your dear forgotten sister?'

'Yes, I know. I'm sorry, but I was too busy: with a World Cup like that one, I couldn't miss a single match; the Sénefs were brilliant. Right now they're in Dakar, but soon they'll be going back to their clubs in France. I so wish…'

'Yes, I know, the same old song. Stop winding me up. You so wish you could come to France. Hurry up and get here, then the Church of Saint-Bernard will be your private mansion. Sure the Sénefs play in France, but that's all you and your friends have learned from that wretched World Cup!'

'Hey, wait! I was about to say I so wish I could see them play live at the Léopold Sédar Senghor stadium in Dakar, for example. Who's talking about leaving? Maybe some of my friends still think about it, but I'm not interested any more. I've got a lot of work in the shop; I'm always having to reorder stock. I think I'm going to build an extension; it's doing really well. I even managed to hire a big TV, and we all watched the World Cup Final at my place. Listen, Grandma wants to know how you are and whether you got her parcel?

She never stops talking about you. She misses you. You really ought to come back home, there's so much to do here.'

I was touched. My voice softened. Back home, love isn't something you declare openly. You have to let it well up from hearts and dig its own channels to flow towards the parched land, like the arms of the Atlantic. You have to sense it behind a person's words, in a fleeting look, a half-smile, a little stroke on the shoulder, in the way they make the last cup of tea last, synchronise their steps when walking someone they love home – things imperceptible from a distance of five thousand kilometres. The slight quaver in my brother's usually steady voice betrayed all that. A baobab doesn't fall to its knees. Telling me that his shop – a stall the size of an upright coffin – was doing well, that his savings were growing, was his way of thanking me. As for Grandma asking after me, even if it were true, that, too, was a roundabout way of telling me, without seeming soft, that he missed me.

'Tell her I'll come soon.'

'I'm not talking about holidays, but about coming back here for good, to your home: your roots must be singing inside you.'

'I like singing, but I'm afraid of wolves.'

'Are you crazy or what? What wolves? We haven't had wolves in the village for ages; and, anyway, there's nothing to stop you moving to the city. At least you'd be with us, back home. I prefer living in my own country, especially now I've got my shop. It's true people buy a lot on credit; some beg outright. The old fisherman, for instance, he's got into the habit of coming and helping himself. But it's OK, we all help each other out. And, anyway, with a bit of money, you can have a good life here. Over there will never really be your home. You should come back. If you had to choose between the two countries, which one would it be?'

'What about you, would you rather have your left leg cut

off or your right arm?' I replied, laughing.

'I don't have to choose,' he answered with a burst of laughter.

'Well, neither do I.'

'Still, you ought to come back: you'll never really be at home there, you know that.'

I wanted to end the conversation on a good note, so I dodged the question and asked him how his little shop was doing and about his plans to extend it. I gave him affectionate messages for every member of the family, knowing full well he wouldn't pass them on. He'd say soberly: 'She says hello, she's fine.'

That's how people talk about those who are far from home, when they've forgotten their favourite food, music, flowers or colour, when people can't remember whether they take sugar in their coffee or not; all those little things that don't fit in a suitcase but which make all the difference between feeling at home when you go back, or not.

Home? Over there? As I am a hybrid, Africa and Europe ask themselves confusedly which bit of me belongs to them. I am the child brought before King Solomon to be cut in equal halves by his sword. A permanent exile, I spend my nights soldering the rails that lead to identity. Writing is the hot wax I pour between the furrows dug by those who erect partitions on both sides. I am that scar that grows where men, marking out their frontiers, have wounded God's land. When, weary of immersion in opaque nocturnal rest, the eye at last desires the shades of day, the sun rises, tirelessly, over colours stolen from the artist's palette to mark off the world. The first one who said 'These are my colours' transformed the rainbow into an atom bomb, and divided peoples into armies. Green, yellow, red? Blue, white, red? Barbed wire? Of course! I prefer mauve, that temperate colour, a mix of African red heat and cold European blue. What makes mauve so beautiful? The blue or the red? And, anyway, what's the use of enquiring whether mauve suits you?

Blue and red, songs and wolves, I've got them on the brain. I carry them with me everywhere. Wherever I go, there'll always be songs and wolves; it's not a question of borders.

I seek my country in places where they appreciate people with complex identities, where there's no need to disentangle their various strands. I seek my country where the fragmentation of identity blurs. I seek my country where the arms of the Atlantic meet to form the mauve ink that tells of incandescence and sweetness, the passion for existence and the joy of living. I seek my country on a white page, a notebook that can fit into a travel bag. So, wherever I put down my suitcases, I'm at home. No net can prevent the seaweed of the Atlantic from drifting and drawing its savour from the waters it traverses. Scraping, sweeping the ocean depths, dipped in squid ink, writing life on the crests of the waves. Let the wind that sings of my seafaring people blow; the ocean cradles only those it calls. I have no mooring. Departure's the only horizon open to those who seek the many caskets where fate hides the solutions to its many errors.

Amid the roar of the paddles, when the mammy-mummy murmurs, I hear the sea declaim its ode to the children fallen overboard. Leave, live freely and die, like seaweed in the Atlantic.

Glossary

Abbé Pierre was the founder of the Emmaus charity homes (the equivalent of Salvation Army hostels), and a lifelong supporter of the homeless and socially disadvantaged.

Bâ, Mariama (1929–81), a Senegalese writer much influenced by Islamic beliefs and traditional customs, whose work combines the political and the personal, she is considered a pioneer of feminism.

Bismillah – 'in the name of God' – invokes a blessing on an action or undertaking of a Muslim.

Bissap Hibiscus-flower tea

Boubou Long loose-fitting garment

Church of Saint-Bernard In August 1996 illegal African immigrants sought protection from deportation in the Eglise Saint-Bernard in Paris. The church was stormed by riot police.

Césaire, Aimé Born in 1913 in Martinique, Césaire became a politician, poet and dramatist and was chiefly responsible for launching the concept of Negritude in reaction to the cultural oppression of the French colonial system.

Chicken yassa A chicken stew with lemon

de Coubertin, Baron Pierre Frédy (1863–1937) was responsible for instigating the modern Olympic Games. He considered sport essential to mental energy.

Djembe A West African drum believed to have come from the Malinke people in the north-east of Guinea. Covered in goatskin, it produces a sharp, bright sound and is used by healers and storytellers, and for accompanying dance and communicating between villages.

Fata of Morgana A mirage of a castle, half in the air and half in the sea, which caused sailors who mistook it for a safe harbour to be lured to their deaths.

Fortune, George The first professor of what is now the Department of African Languages and Literatures at the University of Zimbabwe. He has written widely on the languages of central and southern Africa.

Fremont, Jean A Frenchman who built his own home-made television in the early days of its invention.

Guelwaar Noble warrior

Kora A stringed instrument played in the westernmost part of Africa. It is made from half a calabash covered with cowhide. A traditional kora has twenty-one strings.

La Guele-Tapée is a district of Dakar. Also a pun: gueule = mouth, taper = hit.

Mbalax is the national pop style of Senegal that emerged in the 1970s. It is made up of complex rhythms and usually sung in Wolof, a return to roots after the influence of Calypso and Latin music. Hence the dance.

Pagne Length of cotton which the women wrap around their hips

Quinqueliba tea A local fermented non-alcoholic beverage. When it has boiled to a certain level, it sparkles and makes explosive rumbling sounds when the pot is uncovered.

Sabador Kaftan

Schoelcher, Victor Nineteenth-century slave abolitionist.

Sembere, Ousmane Senegalese novelist and the first film director from an African country to achieve international recognition.

Senghor, Léopold Sédar (1906–2001), Senegalese poet and statesman, elected President of Senegal in the 1960s. With Aimé Césaire, he was one of the originators of the concept of Negritude, defined as the literary and artistic expression of the black African experience.

Sonacotra National society of hostels for immigrants in France

Thiaya Traditional baggy trousers

Thiéboudjène Rice and fish

Toubab White person

Yourcenar, Marguerite (1903–87), a French poet, translator, essayist, historian, critic and novelist, she was an early feminist and great traveller.